DADHÁ AND THE XIBAL VILLAGE

Maximiliano Médici

Cristian Médici

MAGIC REALISM

BARKERBOOKS

Foreword
Gertrudis Médici

This is, without a doubt, the singular story of a family's daily life and a mystical, magical world in which all kinds of Dadaist elements coexist. This movement emerged many years ago, inviting us to delight in the characteristic Dadaist design with shapes, colors, and even the narrative itself sustained by the strength of anti-art and its opposition to positivism.

This work could be defined as a sui generis narration in which the perfect circumstances arise so that the characters and their environments seem to us not only beautiful and intriguing but also disturbing and precious.

It is a work that invites us to understand how magical and non-magical worlds can coincide in one thing: beauty is born from within. This enchantment sometimes has mysterious, deformed, dark, and bitter aspects, but everything the light touches is beautiful, especially when shapes and figures accompanying the blessed dance of fantasy are unveiled.

1

1918

"Tie Captain up well; a rope is not enough. If you won't lock it up, you'd better tie it well with a thick rope." But no, Jacinto thought his friend, the African goat, would behave itself.

After a long voyage and listening to the calls to the captain to the point of exhaustion, he decided to call the goat that had been given to him days before in Guinea "Captain" for two reasons: the captain and owner of the boat, Don Nicolás Martínez Cavaleiro, was very kind to them, and the gentleman and guide of the ship, like the goats, ate everything that came out of the sea.

"You look like a goat; you eat everything," said the young Guinean, brother of Salomé, a beautiful woman who accompanied him on the journey. She had worked for fifteen years to "buy her freedom," which she had lost due to her father's debts. Now, they were traveling to America in search of opportunities.

The pilot's boat, "La Gertrudis," a shallow-water vessel designed to ply the calm waters of the Mediterranean, was making its last voyage across the Atlantic and would henceforth be dedicated to the coastal trade between small ports. A powerful Catalan-built steamer would replace it. The Galician immigrant who owned the boat lived with his family in Isla Mujeres. He owned a large part of the island and an islet attached to the land just in front of the strip of land rich in small coves with reefs and marine life.

Upon reaching land, Salomé decided she did not want to live on an island without schools for her little brother's sake. After asking the Galician about other options, he told her that the next port of call would be Puerto Progreso, where he would deliver merchandise and three tons of cobblestones and rails and load another three tons of henequen bales. He told her that although that port was small, a flourishing city with Spanish and French reminiscences, Mérida was only nineteen miles away, about six hours by platform or cart, and where she would find schools and job opportunities.

Salomé did not think twice, and after agreeing, not without arguing with her brother, who was in love with the Caribbean Sea, they asked him how much it would cost to take them there since they no longer had any money. The good man told Jacinto.

"Look, I know you call that ugly goat Captain in my honor, and a namesake and a beautiful woman are not denied passage. I propose that your sister cooks for us these two days, you clean the decks and my cabin, and we'll be even."

Salomé pampered the palates of the crew and travelers with African and Spanish stews while Jacinto devoted himself to thoroughly cleaning the decks and especially the captain's cabin. There, crumpled and balled up, he found an old and tarnished captain's cap under a trunk. When he asked Don Nicolas about the find, he told him.

"Give it a wash; it is yours, you have earned it." Jacinto asked if he could put it on the goat because it was the captain. After a laugh, the man replied that he should be careful because those animals ate everything.

Two days later, in the afternoon, the ship arrived on the Yucatan coast and anchored a few hundred meters from the shore. When questioned about this event, the captain told them.

"This is a shallow-water coast; we need to transfer to small shallow-draft vessels from here. It will be dark soon. Tomorrow, they will come to transport passengers and load and unload cargo. When you get ashore, look for someone to take you to Mérida. Maybe you'll be lucky."

But their luck, although good, was not good enough. A strong and persistent *"Chiquinic"* wind began to blow at night. This kept them anchored and seasick for two days. When finally, a barge was encouraged to take them ashore along with half a dozen passengers, there were only a couple of platforms with henequen bales waiting for the bad wind to die down.

The other passengers opted to stay at a small inn, but they no longer had any money, and, on top of that, no one welcomed them with a goat. Finally, walking along the shore when the wind began to die down and the afternoon became pleasant, Salomé saw the platforms and a man lying on the bales while a couple of farmhands were lowering the load. Without hesitation, the woman approached the foreman and asked about their destination in a mixed French, African, and some poor Spanish accent.

The foreman replied, "We are headed towards the Xibalbá Hacienda, where we come from. The boss is waiting for us along with his goods, so we must hurry. Why do you ask?"

She replied, "I need to get to Mérida to find work and to put my little brother in a school so he can learn numbers and letters."

"Look," replied Brígido, the foreman, "They are going to bring down some groceries and about ten tracks of rails, as well as some platform wheels from the ship you arrived on and from that other one," he said, pointing to a steamer, "there are some goods and

French tiles from New Orleans, oh! And the coffee with chicory, which is the only one Don Chano drinks. If I arrive without it, he will be very upset. If you wait until we load, we will take you to the hacienda, and there you can ask the boss if he can take you to Mérida. Do you know how to cook?"

"Yes, Spanish, African, and some French food. I worked in Guinea for a restaurant for fifteen years. Give me what you have, and I'll make you a feast," she replied proudly.

"Talk to Don Chano; he needs a new cook because his cook, Doña Mari, is very old and can't see well and sometimes even confuses salt with sugar and has already set the stove on fire twice without realizing it. Now, look for a place to lie down because this will take a long time." And indeed, when the sunset dazzled the newcomers with its spectacular colors, they took the last package up to the platform. Brígido offered them oil with tobacco to repel mosquitoes. Three hours later, completely exhausted, they arrived at the hacienda and began to unload.

Brígido lodged the young Guinean woman and her son in his thatched hut, where five hammocks were already hanging, putting two more for his guests on the second floor. That night, Brígido's wife, Josefina, served them beans with tortillas, something unknown to the newcomer, and sweet bread with freshly made pozole. After dinner, she showed them where the well was so they could clean themselves, and soon after, they fell into a deep sleep, forgetting the goat that, poorly tied, ate the thin rope and, strolling freely, found the door of the main house open.

At that time, Don Eduardo Solís Lucientes, owner and lord of those lands, was cooling off from the heat with tamarind water, remembering his origin and the origin of his wealth: a stroke of luck that had turned him, overnight, from a silver peso into lord and master of that small fiefdom.

Years before, he had arrived in Mérida with his father from a place always kept secret. After completing some formalities, he obtained some identity papers after having "lost" his documents. When the person in charge of the Civil Registry asked his name and accepted a couple of silver pesos to "speed up" the process, he took the name Eduardo. Eduardo Solís Sotelo. And his son, Eduardo Solís Lucientes, after his supposedly deceased mother. He smiled, thinking how clever his father was.

He took a long gulp of saliva and maintained his reverie. He remembered that his luck had changed the day he met Candelaria in the church. Chano was in the process of storing the fifth box of Elixir Paregorico by Stickney & Poor Co. in the pharmacy's back room when Don Eleuterio Gómez, the person in charge of the pharmacy, instructed him to go and put up an advertisement for the recently arrived medicine from the United States. To do so, he gave him the copper plate with the photograph and the text of this magical remedy that stopped diarrhea almost immediately and was eagerly awaited in Mérida because the heat had triggered the cases of dysentery. Before leaving, Don Eleuterio said proudly, pointing to the medicine shelf with the powerful natural extracts.

"Here, dear Chano, is the arrival of the future, the advance of medical science."

The young man, dressed in an old white suit, took the delivery man's bicycle and quickly—dodging the excrement of horses, barouches, and pedestrians—arrived at the newspaper's reception, where he waited a few minutes before being attended. After agreeing that the ad should be on an inside page in a sixteenth size, he paid for the publication, took the day's newspaper, and returned to the pharmacy. On that occasion, his employer overlooked the newspaper, and Chano, during the lunch hour, spent his time skimming through it without much interest. Suddenly, he noticed a small advertisement: *For sale Xibalbá Hacienda in full production, two thousand hectares, furnished farmhouse, machinery. One silver peso. First to arrive at two o'clock in the afternoon.* Chano laughed at what he considered a mistake, "It must be worth a million silver pesos," he said to himself. He turned the page, and a gust of wind that came from who knows where—because everything was closed— brought the page back to his eyes with the small advertisement. He looked at the clock: one forty-five o'clock. After thinking about it for a few seconds, he said to himself, "I want to go and see the surprised faces of the sellers when they see their mistake." He took the copy, got on his bike, and rode to the address about ten blocks away. He arrived at two o'clock and rang the bell. Behind him, a discreet line of well-dressed men began to gather.

Five minutes later, he was sitting in front of an elegant bearded gentleman with a book in front of him and a very distinguished lady next to him. They asked him.

"Are you interested in acquiring the farm? It is free of encumbrances; in fact, the warehouses are full and everything else that the ad says and more."

"But," stammered Chano, "there must be a mistake in the price."

The lady raised her hand and asked.

"Do you have a silver peso to buy it?"

"Yes," answered the incredulous pharmacy assistant. "I have it here, in small change, but I do have it all.

"Will you buy the hacienda with all its contents, free of charge, for one silver peso? Yes or no, other people are waiting," she said, a bit exasperated.

The pharmaceutical clerk took a breath and nodded firmly, with a "what have I got to lose?" look on his face.

In that act, the notary asked him for his general information, registered the information in the protocol, and asked him for the money, to which Chano shakily agreed. The notary gave him the receipt after telling him.

"You are already the owner and responsible for Xibalbá Hacienda and all its assets. It is free of encumbrances. You become, at this moment, responsible for everything that is there. I tell you that the hacienda is very profitable and that the debts of the workers in the *tienda de raya*[1] to you are forty thousand pesos, money that they will never be able to pay because they earn less than they spend, but that money corresponds to you and makes you, in fact, their obligated employer. As long as they owe you, no landowner, by the 'gentleman's agreement,' will give them work. I repeat, you are the owner and responsible for everything there. Here, we conclude."

The lady just smiled and was about to say goodbye, but first, she commented dryly.

"The keys to the main house," she said, handing him a thick ring with a dozen large keys.

The notary, who had written everything in the booklet, said to him as he handed him some papers.

"The operation is completed, Mr. Eduardo Solís. Ah, the checkbook! The bank will inform you of the balance upon presentation of this deed. You're all set now. You can head outside and take possession of your hacienda. You'll find a barouche that belongs to you waiting outside, which will take you to San Jacinto. From there, you can catch a ride to your land on a platform with employees. Just let them know when you're ready to go. Enjoy. You are free to go and, if you please, kindly say goodbye to the other buyers who arrived after you."

---

[1] It was a store located inside the large haciendas and factories where workers could acquire the products necessary for their survival. Then, the masters took advantage of these stores to recover all the money spent on salaries.

Chano went out to the street where there were about five gentlemen and told them.

"I have already bought it; you may leave."

However, he was dying of curiosity after such a bargain. He rang the doorbell again and asked to speak to the couple again. This time, he found them sitting with a well-dressed but more modestly dressed woman across from them.

"Don Eduardo, did you forget something?"

"It's just that," the young man stammered, "I don't understand why it is so cheap."

"Look," said the lady, a little angry, "I'm not used to talking about this subject, but well, I'll make an exception. "My husband, Don Juan Díaz de Regil, has just died. In his will, he left me all his inheritance except... the hacienda you just bought. He left that place to this lady, his "scheming" half-sister who always turned him against me, with the instruction that I should sell it publicly at the price I considered fair, in silver, give her the proceeds, and that is what I have done. Here is the lady, and notice that I can use your presence because I need a witness."

The notary, Don Roberto López Orca, got up from his chair, read a couple of paragraphs in which he repeated what the lady had said, and extended his hand to the "second inheritor" with a receipt that she should sign to receive the amount that corresponded to her. He then handed her the silver weight in small change, and only then did the fine lady address the woman.

"I have fulfilled my shameless husband's wish; now get out of this, my house, take your things, and leave, you opportunistic troublesome ex-sister-in-law!"

Before retiring and after seeing the disconsolate woman leave, Doña Eustaquia said to him.

"Remember, you are responsible for everything there, everything and everyone, including the child Manlio, my late husband's brother, who lives there and suffers from some defects. Don't throw him out; that is a personal request."

Upon leaving the house, the new landowner went to the bank to inquire about the account the notary had given him. Upon seeing the balance, he paled and sat down before the worried gaze of the manager, who, after asking about his health, asked him if he was from Yucatán. Chano looked at the check again and answered.

"Apparently, now Yucatan is mine."

And remembering that fortunate moment, he fell asleep until he felt a strong tug on his hair. He opened his eyes without knowing what was happening and saw a being smiling at him. He immediately thought of the *huay chivo*, a feared underworld being, and began to scream. He turned up the intensity of the lamp, and sure enough, there was a strange red goat on his bed. The most terrifying thing was its smile. It had human-like teeth, but except for that and the stench, it didn't look like what he had heard about the mythical evil entity. He tried to shoo it away, but the goat had climbed onto the bed and was chewing the feather pillow with singular glee. Cautiously, Don Chano slipped over to the window where he had the shotgun and, without thinking, shot the animal in the backside, which, after kicking in the air and emitting loud bleats, jumped up and shot out of the room. "Well," Don Chano said to himself, "this time, it would only burn hits legs for a few days; since it was a mustard ammunition for quails, it was lucky. Where did that critter come from?"

A few minutes later, Brígido arrived, running with Salomé and Jacinto. After questioning him about the visitors, Don Chano told them what had happened and showed them the hole the animal had left in his head.

The newcomer told him she wanted to go to Mérida and had heard she needed a cook. She asked him to put her to the test, and Don Eduardo, still upset, asked her.

"Is that goat yours?"

Jacinto fearfully raised his hand, and after taking a breath, he let it go.

"It's mine; I forgot to tie it properly and it bit the rope."

"Well, let's see. Brigido," said the boss, "you are punished; we'll see what we'll do with you. You can't bring strangers and even less wild beasts onto my property without my authorization. You, little boy, will take the consequences of this injury, so the goat is mine because it is on my ranch; Brigido, grab it and take it to the corrals. As for you, woman, you have no choice but to work in my house to pay me for the animal's damage, look!" Only then did they realize that the goat had broken vases, stained glass windows and nibbled all the elegant bedding in its mad rush.

That same night, in Merida, Chano's cantankerous brother-in-law, Candelaria's younger brother Juanra, had a dream after learning the news that he would be a father.

He saw himself in a white corridor full of windows with dozens of newborn children all crying. At the end, in the center of the hallway, he saw a large window surrounded by a churrigueresque golden frame splashed with colorful paint with a large sign at the top that read *MÉDICI*. Little by little, he approached the window that bore his last name, baiting the babies who were crying at the top of their lungs, and found a pink room full of pink pompoms and a newborn baby girl dressed in black, who was not crying but laughing. When she saw him, she threw her arms out to which Juanra fanned with the cane, shouting, "This is a Dadaist scene, this is Dadaist!" and continued shouting until he fell out of bed on the chamber pot which, at that time, was full of urine. After shouting his bad luck, he promised himself to call the unborn child Dadhá if it turned out to be a girl.

Very early in the morning, while Don Chano was still sleeping at the hacienda, doña Candelaria, his wife, in Mérida, was already on her way after breakfasting some eggs with chaya and onion, a dozen tortillas, a chocolate with water and three pieces of good bread, to celebrate holy mass. That day, she lamented, she would not be able to receive communion, but her appetite won out. When her husband did not sleep at home, she became nervous and drank orange blossom infusions of bitter orange and mint for her nerves. It was a Mayan recipe of her cook Mari that she drank almost like water. That morning, she hurriedly drank two cups of the "magic" tea after breakfast.

Dawn was breaking when the woman, who was a few minutes late, walked hurriedly with her three maids, all dressed in black, in front of her. The obese woman, wearing a thick black dress—blacker than those of her maids who were dyed—down to her ankles, of fine, thick fabrics and a Spanish mantilla that covered her face, repeated to herself, "The visit to the house of the Lord begins at home." and alternated her saying with "Hail Marys." She carried a fine olive wood rosary in her right hand, brought by the bishop from the very Mount of Olives, which he gave to Candelaria for her permanent contributions to the seminaries and convents. The event in which the sacred instrument was given to her was one of the happiest days of her life. She recalled the ceremony after the Tridentine Mass, at the beginning of the Advent season, where the most distinguished members of society, the ladies of the Catholic Action and their husbands, witnessed the delivery of the sacred garment, preceded by a few words of the bishop who had just arrived from the Holy Land.

"Candelaria," he affirmed emotionally, "is a refuge of faith, a fortress of the poor, a woman of God and of the Church. She will be a saint!"

Inwardly, during the ceremony, Candelaria recalled how far she had climbed up the social ladder since leaving her small village, Dzonot, where she was born to the union of an Italian sailor and a mixed-race mother, in a small thatched house with eleven half-siblings and a little brother. Fleeing from her origin, Candelaria took refuge in a convent as a kitchen maid, from where she was taken out because of her propensity to overeat. She, with forty-four extra pounds, being expelled from what she thought was paradise after a lifetime of deprivation and hunger, escaped from the cloister because they wanted to put her to wash floors. She went to the cathedral to pray to find a home, and she was so lucky that that day, the young pharmacist who used to bring the remedies to the convent was kneeling with his hands to the sky as an act of giving thanks and when he finished his prayers, he fixed his eyes on her. He waited for her in the atrium to greet her and introduce himself. She smiled her best smile, and a few months later, after telling him that she was an Italian immigrant from Florentine society who had been losing her Italian due to lack of practice, they were married in the absence of her family and with the sole presence of some nun friends. As time went by, she herself believed in her noble origins and became, twenty years later, a completely different woman.

In her left hand, the sturdy woman carried a wrought iron cane, topped by a silver cross, which she did not need to walk but to bait the poor girls forced to wear their heads covered with scratchy sisal cloth, dyed black as a mantilla, which made them itch because of its roughness. They could not talk to each other during the journey, or they would receive a scolding from their pious mistress. As if that were not enough, their "dresses" were fiber sacks, also dyed black, "Because it is not worth spending a *potosí*[2] to dress three infidels who God knows if they have souls."

That early morning, a man from the street, walking along the creek, approached her, asking for money. Candelaria, in one swift movement, gave the daring man a severe blow to the back of the head and shouted at him.

"Insolent, vicious, someday you're going to hell, but today I'm going to give you a taste of what is waiting for you!" The man stared her in the eyes, hurting from the blow, and staggered away from the dizziness caused by the impact.

Upon waking up in his hacienda, Chano went to the dining room, where the table was already set. A tablecloth embroidered with multicolored flowers in cross stitch and a set of dishes made in Ticul especially for the family in pink clay with his seal in the center, along with fine German silverware, a pitcher of chinalima juice, and a platter of papaya awaited him.

Josefina, the usual cook, asked him what he would have for breakfast, to which he answered without hesitation.

"Four eggs with sausage, French bread brought to me from progress, my refried beans, and my coffee with chicory."

"By the way, do you know if my coffee arrived from New Orleans?"

Josefina, sparing in speech except when there was news, told him.

"Yes, of course, your order arrived as you requested, but I have news for you. The workers told us that three suspects of a disease they call 'influyemza,' which is like a very strong flu but Spanish, were on the ship and that two sailors died of it on the trip here.

---

[2] A fortune. Extraordinary or very great wealth.

Today, they were going to take the sick to the hospital. They were waiting for someone to take them."

"Let them sit and wait. Let the health service take them. They will not be received if they pass through here, lest they become contagious. Moreover, no stranger enters the hacienda until I arrive in Mérida and find out what it is all about. By the way, did the young Guinean girl and her brother come on that boat?"

"No, Don Chano. She came from Isla Mujeres; she knows nothing about the disease. The plague ship is the American steamer."

"Ah, that's perfect because no strangers are coming in. Put some buckets of water next to the rails in case they need water, but that's all; don't come near them. The hacienda is closed until further notice. Nobody goes out either, and if they do, they won't come back in, except for me, who will take care of myself. When I get to Mérida, I will buy the national press to see if there is any news. Tell your husband the hacienda is closed until I give the order."

The next day, Brígido informed him that those transporting the sick had asked for asylum but were told there were hospitals in Mérida. They insisted, but the workers refused to open the gate. They were only provided with water for their mules and a small amount for themselves to drink.

"Nobody approached; everything from a distance, as you told us."

"Tell them to stand guard in threes all night long, lest they force their way in," Don Chano told him.

When the full moon illuminated the hacienda with all its splendor, the environment shone faintly and magically. Filemón dozed, leaning on some bales of shredded and combed henequen. The hunter stared at the moon with a glazed look, and Filemón's son, Filito, was attentive to everything happening.

At about three o'clock in the morning, Filito felt the presence of someone. He sharpened his eyes and saw a shadow on the sidewalk leading to the cornfield, and an indescribable scent enveloped him. He had a second look, and a female figure appeared clearly in the distance. He looked again, and it seemed to him that it was one of Brígido's daughters. He excused himself to the guard, saying he was going to pee, and headed towards the figure, moving away as the boy approached. And he began the race to catch up with the woman. From the main path, there were others where the young woman got lost. A pebble hit his left cheek, and the young man took a left turn. Three times, the same thing happened. Right, then left. Finally, he reached the cenote hidden behind large trees that drank from it and saw the woman clearly. She was the most beautiful woman his eyes had ever beheld. She jumped into the water, and Filito followed her. The young woman was already under a leafy tree when he looked for her inside the small space illuminated by the moon's rays. With the agility that only youth provides, he jumped out in two leaps and caught her. She was not Brígido's daughter, whom he had been romancing for days. She was a beautiful goddess; he took her in his arms and kissed her. When the moon went down, the smell of flowers turned, to the young man's horror, into a pestilent scent of sulfur. Only then did he understand.

In the morning, Chano visited Manlio, who was locked in the back room, looking at the window and laughing as if he was talking to someone. Trying to converse with the young man, who was distracted by what Chano thought was some imaginary being, a woman he knew came in, screaming in dismay.

"Don Chano, Don Chano, they found my son under a ceiba tree, without eyes, dead. He was standing guard as you ordered, and he went away to *uichar* and never came back... his body has the smell of hell; it was the Ixtabay! Help us!"

The landowner, not fully believing her claims and thinking it was just a boy's quarrel, took three pesos and gave them to the woman to make a coffin. He told her to go to the store and ask for another two pesos of groceries for the wake and left, promising to attend some prayer.

While the wake was being held in the afternoon, he arrived, put a coin over each empty socket, made the sign of the cross, and refused a plate of chocolomo on his way out. He had doubts about the Mayan rituals and preferred not to ask.

On Sunday morning, after loading the roofed platform with a double bench in the center, he told Salomé and Jacinto that, unlike the farmhands who had to sit on the floor of the vehicle, armed in case a deer or bandit appeared, they should sit on the bench in the back.

Chano disliked the clothes Candelaria forced him to wear when he was in Mérida and said quietly.

"Wearing a frock coat, wool pants, and a top hat in the middle of summer in Mérida is an ordeal. Someday, I will rebel against this anarchic clothing. Well, at least they keep me from being eaten by mosquitoes that look like bats because of their size."

And so, under a scorching sun, they advanced slowly. The return trip was unbearably long. On two occasions, they had to stop because some rail sections some thieves had taken were missing. *They would be caught and punished,* "the master," thought contritely. In those cases, they had to dismantle a rear section and install it in front so the vehicle could pass. The task took about an hour because a nut from the previous section was rusted, and the employees struggled to remove it, "That's why they didn't take this section," said one of them, "there's no way." Chano complained because, after so much time and heat, there was no more cold fruit water, only ice water. No deer, turkey, or living thing crossed their path this time. Chano described the trip as hellish and calculated it would be forty degrees heat without a drop of air. To make matters worse, a cloud of mosquitoes accompanied them to the entrance of Mérida. That and wearing a frock coat was a torment.

As soon as he arrived, he went to the store that received the capital's newspapers and bought the *Excélsior* and the *Carta Peninsular*, which published some information about the flu, which they called "Spanish influenza." The capital newspaper gave a summary of the pandemic. Officially, there were thirty-four serious cases, and an order had already been issued to interrupt railroad communications with the country's northern border to avoid contagion. There was also talk of some cases, not yet confirmed, in the port of Veracruz and some coastal points along the Gulf of Mexico and the Caribbean Sea. Next to the information, in a highlighted box, there was a note about the person in charge of Health, who had declared, "There is no cause for alarm, as those infected have not shown any signs of serious illness." When reading it, Chano felt relieved that Candelaria would be more concerned about the disease than the arrival of the colored girl and her brother. He advised them not to look Candelaria in the eyes and to try to remain invisible if possible. He promised her that he would see that they were happy. In addition, there were eight other girls they could get along. Salomé would arrive to help Mari before she retired and returned to the hacienda with her family.

When he arrived, he was greeted by his grumpy brother-in-law, who reprimanded him about his absence and his sister's distress at what he called "the beginning of the end of the world." As if in response to his unbearable in-law, Chano handed him the recently purchased newspaper, which the dirty fellow read avidly. Juanra, or Rafita as he was also known, was ugly; he had a huge, crooked, wrinkled nose with a pimple on one side. His ugliness was only eclipsed by his stench. Wearing a shabby, thick morning coat in a city where it was hot as hell all year round, he bathed, if at all, twice a month.

"Never with soap because it burns!" He did this because his wife demanded it when the stench was already unbearable.

Chano arrived and greeted his dear wife from a distance. She was furious and asked him why he was late. A turkey with black stuffing had been prepared in honor of the future parents, and next week, there would be a family meal.

With feigned patience and repressed hatred, Chano politely asked Candelaria about her health, to which she answered as if to complain.

"You'd better ask your sister-in-law; she's already pregnant, and I'm about to have a stroke from so much displeasure. I confronted an Indian with strange eyes who wanted to take money from me, and with this one," she said, pointing to her cane, "I gave him a good beating! And now, stop questioning me and tell me about that pandemic." Chano explained to her what he had read in the Mexican newspaper Juanrá held as he read, picking his nose and cursing paranoidly.

"All this was invented to harm me! Now, I won't be able to go to Mexico to present my book of poems because of this pandemic! And on top of that, I'm going to be a father! I'm not in the mood to hear a baby crying! And what is the midwife going to charge? My God, what am I going to do?"

Chano received all kinds of insults for asking Juanra for the newspaper and reading the news to Candelaria.

"Mexico's health official said there is no reason to be alarmed, as only thirty people have been infected with mild symptoms. However, given the international news, he announced that the borders with the United States were being closed and explained that extreme precautions would be taken in the ports of the Gulf."

"Well, look," said Chano to Candelaria, "a platform passed through the hacienda where a couple of gringo sailors were dying of the flu. It is a disease of dirty people, according to the intellectuals and scientists who write in the newspaper. Ah, look, here come the recommendations. Do not approach the sick, make sure they are clean, wear a mask to not breathe the same air as the infected, and cool your mouth with menthol. The instructions must be carefully observed, he told her. By the way, I hired this girl," he said, introducing Salome, "and her brother." Candelaria instructed Mari to ensure that the newcomers were bathed with Corona soap and then taken to the barracks. She also ordered to burn all their belongings, dress them in the clothes left behind by a couple who had gone to seek their luck in Campeche, provide them with an old hammock, and check their hair to prevent a lice and nit infestation.

"I imagine," Candelaria finished, "that those foreigners will be heretics; they will have to be converted. The difficult thing is to get God into their heads. Let's hope they don't start with strange rituals. I won't allow that."

"Well, Candita," said Chano, "I am going to call Dr. Saturnino Laviada, Don Maximiliano Acosta, and my friend Martin Medina, owner of the famous apothecary shop 'The Good Remedy,' to an emergency meeting to deliberate at length on the subject of the strange disease. We will decide what action to take and, if necessary, draft a letter to Governor Carrillo Puerto to urge him to observe our recommendations. Please order coffee with chicory to be prepared; it is an important meeting. Oh, and have butter cookies prepared for me," he said with a certainty that was gradually erased from his face by the annoyed face of Candelaria, who already had her cane in her hand.

"Cookies?" asked Candelaria angrily. "I'm going to give you your 'cook-ies,' you scoundrel; they already told me that you are without a frock coat at the hacienda. I can't stop praying for your lost soul!"

Chano hunched over and laughed nervously. Without turning his back on her, he withdrew, walking backward, keeping a close eye on the iron cane Candelaria held out threateningly and repeating in a trembling voice.

"Candi, Candi, it's just that they envy me for being married to you-"

"Look, get out of my sight; I feel bad. I plan to drink my magical tea before bed and soak in a bath with plum leaves to soothe my rash and rest. This northern weather is awful for me. It's better to sleep."

Chano smiled to himself in relief. After a long bath, he went to his cool office to wait for his colleagues, whom he immediately greeted and told.

"My dear Martin, Saturnino, and Maximiliano, today we are facing a health emergency that, it seems, will be worldwide. As moral representatives of society, we must take action on the matter."

His interlocutors were dressed in 19th-century style: frock coats and vests, some with pocket watches, monocles, linen handkerchiefs, and the occasional cane. They were seated in comfortable rocking chairs and wore affected expressions.

Dr. Acosta intervened.

"This disease is actually produced by a bacillus, which is why we commonly call it influenza. It arose, according to my sources, at Fort Riley in the United States, where more than five hundred soldiers have died. That is where it comes from, and here it arrives by sea. I was informed that there are already five cases in the Mérida hospital of people who had contact with infected sailors coming from New Orleans.

"That's right," said Chano, "I witnessed it on my hacienda."

They all leaned back protectively, and the host remarked.

"Don't worry. This disease, say some doctors in the capital, is due to dirt. If infected people meet with dirty people, they get sick. I stayed at least fifty meters away from them, and when I saw them, I took a bath with fragrant flowers and rubbed myself with orange tree cologne."

After the doctors' admiring assent, they continued their deliberations. Martin said bluntly.

"The governor must be required to isolate the affected people after bathing them. And everything, including the streets, must be washed with creolin."

"That and gargling with hydrogen peroxide and menthol," said Maximiliano, the doctor.

Saturnino, who had remained silent, proposed writing the letter, and Chano, who had a reputation for good handwriting, took out a quality piece of paper. Together, they all contributed ideas, advice, and demands, including that anyone found dirty should be bathed, shaved, and confined for observation.

Almost at the end, Maximiliano recommended that the entire domestic service be subjected to a thorough bath and forced to use a mouth cover with four layers of grease. He offered to send the gadgets' design and way of manufacture in the morning.

Once the deliberations were concluded and with the tranquility of the declarations of the Mexican government's health official, in the sense that "there is nothing to worry about," they drank their last coffee with chicory, very rare to find and therefore very celebrated, without knowing that, in three months, almost four percent of the Mexican population would die of the terrible disease and then disappear. At that time, there was talk of entire towns full of dead people in the center of the country in the face of governmental indifference. After the meeting, he took advantage of Candelaria falling deeply asleep when she drinks her tea and takes her bath. So, he instructed all the servants to go out to the yard and take a bath at that moment.

After the unexpected nighttime cleaning, the women put on clean clothes and lined up, plate in hand, as they did every night, at the doors of Chano's office. Aware of the frugal dinner they were receiving on Candelaria's orders, Chano took on the task of giving them an extra ration. He took a mortadella and a big ham knife and shouted, "Dinner time!" And everyone was happy.

For the next three months, the girls had to wear the mask with the repulsive smell of three baits: cow, sheep, and pork. Those were difficult days when the house's inhabitants did not go out, and some things from the quality pantry, such as American coffee or Dutch cheeses, were scarce.

There was no shortage of food thanks to Chano, who brought corn and pork, salted fish, pibil deer meat, and wild turkeys from the hacienda. They also sacrificed an old ox; the meat was selected, and the best was sent to the main house, while the tails, ears, head, and entrails were distributed among the starving workers. Fortunately, there were no contagions in Xibalbá, thanks to the owner's instructions not to meet with people from other haciendas, not to deliver henequen to the ships, and to adopt the use of masks under penalty of being banned from the store. For his part, the owner provided them with a roll of coarse cloth and the mixture of baits, unlike some nearby haciendas that did not adopt the hygienic measure and continued exporting and infecting themselves. Red flags were placed at the entrance to these farms.

Everyone in the Medici household was happy except for Jacinto. His friend "Captain" was no longer around, as Chano had left with some ammunition that needed to be removed, causing the goat to cry. Although the ammunition was not dangerous, it still needed to be taken care of. That and the fact that its immaculate fur was stained with blue ink—methyl violet—made the young boy angry. One morning, while telling Felipa, Brígido's youngest daughter, who was helping her father pay off the *tienda de raya* debt, she had an idea. She took Jacinto by the hand and led him to the back of the yard.

"Look," she said, "this tree is a huachín tree, and whoever rubs on its leaves or takes its fruit ends up colís, without a hair. I've seen many horses go bald from eating it. I have an idea." She continued, "If we climb the tree and take some fruit and some tender leaves, we'll make Don Chano bald," she said while laughing.

In the afternoon, both Don Chano and Doña Candita would get a boiling bucket of plum leaves to relieve the itching caused by the clothes they wore. She was in charge that the water for Doña Candelaria should be ready at six o'clock and at seven o'clock for Don Chano. So she proceeded with her plan: plum water for the mistress, huachín water for the master. The plan went perfectly. In the morning, Jacinto squeezed ten or more fruits from the toxic plant into the water container, which only Don Chano drank. Doña Candita and the others only liked kumquat orange water. And the plan turned out better than expected. That day, the master woke up thirstier than usual and drank one glass after another until he finished the refreshing juice pitcher. The rest was to observe how, day after day, strands of hair fell from the head of the one who dared to strip Jacinto of his most precious asset.

2

"Mari, Mariiiiiiiiii...! Bring me my cough drops and a magic tea, the one with bitter orange blossom and mint; I feel nervous! Mariiiiiii! God alone knows how I suffer for you, Chano!" exclaimed the thick woman, dressed from the neck down to the floor, totally in black and accompanied only by her pet, a lizard of two and a half meters and fearsome jaws that she had named Justino and that wandered freely around the main house. She used to scare the young employees by saying, "He attacks those who betray me, so keep that in mind." She looked at her husband and continued, "Chano, I can't stand your habit of attending these small-town festivities anymore. I'm telling you this without anger. To come and tell me that you'll spend the afternoon at the circus theater watching a mock bullfight is just too much for me. Chanito, what kind of taste do you have?" she said dramatically. "But here I will wait for you... praying for your soul and that you don't catch the Influenza and leave me a widow!" She shouted again, "Mariii!"

The spacious room, featuring a stunning central courtyard and another one measuring a hundred meters, is part of an 18th-century residence in the heart of Mérida. It was purchased outright by Chano when he got married. This room was the setting for what happened next. María Candelaria Medici de Solís, a woman of God, guardian of good manners, lady of society, and to whom no one ever held her gaze, suffered a convenient dizzy spell and went tilting on the palm weaving armchair that resisted, creaking in between, when the more than three hundred pounds spilled over the oldest piece of furniture in the house, that "If I don't survive this, I want you to sell it to Juanrá at half price because he is the only brother who really loves me.... even if he doesn't show it! I can't think of our Christian home falling into the wrong hands. Mari, my menthol pills and my tea!"

After the entertaining mock bullfight, where a bull chased the clowns and the audience until it bumped into them in a circus theater full of people, some of whom were aristocrats wearing masks, Don Eduardo felt rejuvenated. It was good for him to share it with his friends, among them Max, who, in his excitement, had already taken off his frock coat and, with his big belly in the air, was laughing like a child.

"So, Chano, how was your show?" said Candelaria, puffing up her nose like a wild beast before attacking. "Was it fun enough?"

The thin man, sweating and impeccably dressed, according to the etiquette of the time, replied, fanning himself with a handkerchief as if he smelled some perfume.

"Oh Candita, it was very exhilarating and fun, and the people were so excited! More than a hundred were denied entry because they looked dirty or sick; they caused an unpleasant spectacle! I can't even tell you; it went on for hours. Very tiring, that's for sure. Next time, I'd listen to you and stay with you 'to enjoy' the afternoon. I have already ordered a new Emerson radio, which will soon be delivered and we can enjoy the entertaining programmes. Modernity has arrived."

"Don't change the subject," she replied angrily. "The servant told me you arrived at eleven thirty! I didn't wait for you because that tea makes me sleepy. It's too late for a man of your standing to be walking around alone. I'm sure you went to Max's house to play dominoes," the enraged wife lashed out as she could no longer hide her conjectures. "And in the middle of a pandemic!"

Making an effort, Chano faced Candelaria's claim with acrimony.

"I do not allow you, for any reason or by any means, to doubt my honorability, and I can't stand being watched by the servant!"

Then, gathering his strength, he took his cane and went to his study without breakfast and with trembling legs. He sat down in his armchair in front of the "secretaire desk" where he kept the accounts of his estate, unbuttoned his tie, and faded into a deep sleep.

Candelaria, for her part, looked everywhere, and as she had no audience, she did not faint and just shouted to Mari, her housekeeper and cook, for her breakfast and pills.

"Linda, bring me some motuleño eggs with Spanish ham, good bread, fruit, and china juice. Ah, when you come, bring me the mints, the little green box. But you don't know the colors anymore. Why do I even bother? The green box, because my cough hasn't stopped bothering me all night. It must be my nerves. Make me my tea, too, full of orange leaves; nothing gives me life anymore!"

That Sunday, to Candelaria's chagrin, some of her siblings were expected to visit. In addition, Eugenio Andrade, a friend of the family, accompanied by "that Venezuelan, Maria, a climber, who only wants to live from embassy to embassy, boasting that Eugenio writes very well and that he will become governor," and Loreto, with her husband Carlos, "I don't know what Loreto saw in that railroad worker son of an emigrant who loves to arrive before time."

The house had an orchard full of orange, tangerine, and tamarind trees, and in the background, a fenced chicken coop with some birds and a brand-new white turkey, taking the fresh air without knowing that in a few days, it would be the star of the dinner. Mari's son, Gaspar Xiu, had named it "Coconut Snow" and consoled it by telling it, without being understood, how beautiful death was and that it would not hurt, that it would be like falling asleep.

That day, Dieguito Cifuentes Medici, Loreto's son, began to play with him. Soon after, the owner of the house's scream was heard.

"Those damned brats are screamers, but one of these days, I'll kick them out on the street, along with those half-dressed little girls with those horrendous huipiles[3]. Mariii! Bring me my tea, and please dress those girls well or have their mother take care of them. Can't you see their exposed chests?"

The "girls" in question were three and four years old. Chano curiously asked his "beloved" Candi, "Who do you talk to when you talk to yourself?" She answered sarcastically.

"With the only thinking person in this madhouse: myself."

The restless nephew ran around the house and drank a lot of water. Playing with Gaspar, Maria's son, he would steal pieces of cheese and bread to share with him. At one unfortunate moment, the still beloved nephew, only seven years old, felt the urge to pee, and being in the yard, he did it right there, with such bad luck that the owner of the house, guardian of decency and the fear of God, saw him, and exclaiming with Yucatecan fury some expletives, said to Loreto.

"Look, sis, you can come to this house whenever you want, and you can even bring that railroader, but Dieguito never again, he dared, without any modesty, to urinate in the yard!"

---

[3] The word huipil comes from the Nahuatl word huipilli, which means blouse or ornate dress. The use of this is considered a tradition among indigenous women.

Except for this incident, the highlight of the meal was un-doubtedly the unjustifiable fifteen-minute delay of Eugenio and the Venezuelan woman, as well as the scandal that broke out when he arrived with don Eusebio Escalante aboard the first Ford Model T automobile to travel through Yucatecan lands. People crowded around to admire that strange cart that went without horses, and Candelaria only looked at it with a certain contempt because "I would never ever get into a mass-produced car, I want a Maxwell, one of those that Don Alonsito Escalante announced in the Carta Peninsular that he is going to sell and, he says it is handmade, with fine wood and good iron, like the carriages of the highest quality."

Don Eusebio said during the meal that the day they gave him the car, people made the sign of the cross as he passed, and when he turned the corner of the "Iglesia de Monjas," the parish priest, crucifix in hand, made him stop.

"They had already told me what you had, Don Eu, a carriage that moves with the hidden forces of evil."

"Not at all! They are hidden but not evil!"

Don Javier Molina, the owner of a dozen calash that served as cabs, told the priest almost in secret.

"Some hidden monstrous animal drives them. I demand that you let us inspect it because if so, you will have to ask for a ba-rouche permission! I think there is a dwarf mule in that hood," he said, shaking his head.

The people began to crawl underneath to see if they could see the hooves, until Don Eusebio opened the mysterious front box and they saw that it was a strange noisy engine, like the henequen rasp, but smaller and giving off a lot of smoke, with the smell of petroleum. The priest simply poured holy water on the vehicle, extended his hand to receive charity for the service rendered, and only then allowed it to continue on its way.

Life for Candelaria was very difficult because times were changing so fast. One of her favorite activities was, without a doubt, to meddle in the private lives of others. Thus, in the afternoons, she would sit and watch the carriages, victorias, and calash go by. She had a particular preference for watching what was going on in the funeral parlor, which was, if you were well situated inside the house, "a bird's eye view." That and taking her soothing infusion at the slightest symptom of whatever it was gave her the energy to "bear her cross."

One day, the scandal was huge because when she was about to look outside as she did in the mornings, she noticed that the neighbor across the street, Don Maximiliano Acosta, a surgeon and midwife, a great friend of her husband's, was sitting at the window-door of his house, comfortably dressed.

"Chano, Chano, what indecency!" she shouted in terror, "Don Max is sitting in full view of everyone, in his shirtsleeves and without a frock coat! How horrible!" That same day, the window facing the house was closed and never again opened. Of course, this was reason enough for the shameless doctor's wife to be excluded from social gatherings, and Don Max's consultations were drastically reduced. "I didn't like him for a reason, I was right!" she exclaimed for the next fifteen days, who had ten failed deliveries because she did not allow the doctor to examine her.

For the hot Yucatecan nights, Candelaria, a woman of the highest virtues, never used to sleep in anything simpler than a thick nightgown, as the bad winds of the night could make one sick.

Candelaria jealously guarded her privacy. Chano did not enter her bedroom during the day, only once during a very long illness, hepatitis, which prostrated her for months. Her life was rigid, but deep down, she had a secret, tender, and painful vein caused by the only thing that touched her heart: her lost children. For twenty years, she had ten pregnancies that she carried to term, but her stubbornness was stronger, and death, at the time of delivery, snatched those little guests from the closed and smoked room every two years to wait for them lovingly. She justified herself by saying that the midwife was not capable, and the assistant explained to her that the presence of a doctor was essential at the time of delivery, given her great weight. She always refused, categorically, and she lost them all.

On some quiet afternoons, Candita could be heard humming old lullabies locked in the unborn child's room.

The frustrated mother took good manners to the extreme. One of many days, she went out in her theatrical procession to the cathedral to listen to the six o'clock mass. As always, in front of her, as if they were draft horses, were her three girls with their mantillas on, their masks on, and their heads down. They could not talk to each other or look at anyone! Under penalty of fasting if they were caught. And a young, distracted boy offended her to the core. It turns out that the stripling—without a mask—was in a hurry, and when he met the women, he decided not to get off the sidewalk as he had to and put his back to the wall to let them pass. He continued his accelerated walk, and Candelaria, who had to put one foot on the paving stone, was deeply stunned because "He did not give us the sidewalk! Values and respect have been lost forever; it is the end of civilization." She stood there for a few seconds until, from the bottom of her stomach, she said, "Girls, let's go back home; education is over!" And Candelaria Medici de Solis never left her house again, not even one day of the many years that remained of her life.

The pandemic lasted almost four months. During that time, the girls did not even go out to the store, and only Chano, with a spectacular pelican beak-shaped mouth cover designed by Candelaria inspired by medieval fashion after reading a book about the bubonic plague and with a generalized baldness, went to the hacienda to check the accounts and to check the warehouses. He also liked to observe how the rasping machine worked, which he had already fixed on one occasion when he could not find the mechanic. The day Candelaria proudly handed him the "elegant" face mask, Chano wanted to protest, but the woman told him bluntly.

"If you want to go to the hacienda, wear it and don't take it off! If I find out that you stop wearing it on the way or when you talk to the farmhands, you'll never set foot in this house again. And that's final!"

But I'm going to look like a crow, he thought. The man had to endure the laughter of the people in the street as he rode his barouche to San Jacinto to take his platform to his hacienda. His workers were warned that, at the first laugh, they would not be able to buy at the store for a week. Faced with such a threat, they had to bite their tongues. Some could not stand it and suffered an apparent fast, as their family asked neighbors for help, who invariably provided them with small amounts of food on the sly.

From then on, Chano was given the name X'cau Solís in honor of the species of small crows that abound in Yucatán.

3

Dadhá was born on the first of May. She weighed thirteen pounds and was registered in the midwife's book as the biggest baby girl born up to that moment in the peninsula. At the time of delivery, Dr. Laviada had to perform an episiotomy on Trina, the mother, a technique he had learned in Europe during his last study trip. The baby was so heavy that he had to ask for help to lift her. Days before, the doctor, based on the size of the woman's belly, thought that twins were coming, but he was puzzled when he could only hear one heart. That day, the mystery ended. And another one emerged. The blue-eyed baby girl was born laughing, cackling tenderly, and only cried when she was dressed. That day, Father Avila was summoned, and he showed up in his usual white habit and a black stole since he had just come from a funeral mass in the chapel.

The priest witnessed the sudden change in the baby's behavior as she laughed without clothes on and cried when dressed in white robes. Then, out of the blue, her father, who had come in to see her in a rage over the problem, remembered the dream and said, "Try dressing her in something black." Everyone made the sign of the cross as Juanra told of his dream. Candelaria reluctantly handed over a black silk mantilla, without lace, that she used to wear around the house on saints' days. Putting it on as a diaper,

Dadhá forgot to cry and laughed louder than before, and her smile became adorable. The child never accepted any garment that was not black. Neither as a young girl nor as a woman, nor to get married. Nor to sleep in. Never.

Trina was beside herself when she received the news of her best friend's death and was unable to feed her baby. It had only been a week since Dadhá's birth. Immediately, they set out to find a wet nurse. Two came forward: a white woman from a good family who had just given birth and a large-bodied mestiza who had given birth to twins. Both tried to breastfeed the baby girl, who kept crying from hunger, but she refused the wet nurses. At that moment, it occurred to Trina to tell Doña Nely, the mestiza, to cover her breast with a black cloth, and Dadhá began to eat, and fortunately, despite having twins, she had enough milk for all of them.

The day they dared to say "no" to Dadhá for the first time when she was about to turn six, they learned the extent of the fury of an overindulged child who had turned out to be terribly manipulative. She told them that, at night, she heard voices telling her to go to her uncle's estate, where wonderful things awaited her.

"No, no, and no," said her father, Juanra.

"If you don't let me celebrate my birthday there, I'll go live in the weather vane," Dadhá replied.

Her father refused. He was reluctant to travel in the middle of May to a place five hours away through the mosquito-ridden hills. Only once had he visited Xibalbá, and it was to verify what Chano had told him about the origin and magnitude of his fortune, which he had always envied and suspected. Behind his back, he said it was "ill-gotten money."

The curmudgeon was too worried because a manuscript of a work he had been writing for two months had disappeared the day before. Such was his anger that the next morning, as almost always, he had to run to the bathroom.

"You spill too much bile," Dr. Laviada told him. "Your liver can't keep up with you. You spend your bile on everything but digesting."

"You don't know anything, you shoddy doctor! They're probably poisoning me because the girls hate me; Chano envies me because he doesn't even know how to write his own name, and he has a hacienda that he stole from the owners, and I'll tell him that to his face! He sure is bringing some poison from that damned hell to harm me. Candelaria won't even let me take off my frock coat at noon, and since yesterday I went to bed and went to the bathroom without putting on that thick rag, she threw a terrible tantrum because, according to her, it was wrong!" After venting, he shouted his usual threat, "One day, I'm going to leave, and you'll never see me again!" Then he stood up from the armchair and locked himself in his foul-smelling room, which hadn't been cleaned in a while per his request. He enjoyed the putrid odor.

The night before the refusal, Dadhá had heard that there was no way anyone would go to the hacienda, but Trina confronted her husband.

"I've already told the girl yes, so you tell her no." When she heard them behind the door, the little girl, dressed as always in black with a closed collar, slipped in the dark into the writer's room and stole the manuscript from his bedside table. From what her father told her, it was the revelations—invented—of the intimate life of the rulers. She did not understand what that meant but hid the thick file in her closet.

The next day, upon receiving the refusal, Dadhá did not hesitate; she took the papers, slipped through the bars of her room, climbed the weather vane with the "lost" document, and fifty feet up, began to make a fuss with the blades that were spinning wildly, rubbing them with a wrench. Minutes later, the girls came out to see horrified at the little girl who shouted at them that she would not come down again, but first, she wanted her father to see how she released her work to the wind, shouting that, after throwing the last page, she would settle down to live on the small platform, which caused hysteria among the girls, her mother, and Candelaria who came out only to make the sign of the cross. When the writer went out into the yard, the first thing he saw were about ten pages flying, and he looked at his daughter out of the corner of his eye. He negotiated with her, and they agreed to go to the hacienda if she would stop throwing more pages in the wind and get off the weather vane because she would knock it off level.

The journey to Xibalbá was an odyssey. Wearing a strange hat with a deer's head, Trina covered Dadhá with a hammock canopy hanging from the platform's back roof. The writer sat next to the platformer because he liked the smell of mules. Chano, in front of the front bench, was furious because he would be forced to behave himself, and that included wearing a frock coat in the middle of the bush in a forty-degree weather.

For dinner, onion soup, venison in sour orange, mashed potatoes with Dutch cheese, and for dessert, papaya jam. That night, the eve of Dadhá's birthday, everything went peacefully. Chano was lost all afternoon going through the inventories. Trina and Rafael sat drinking a pitcher of lemonade while they watched Dadhá play with the children of the hacienda. "Let's see if she doesn't get lice," was all the bitter writer said, fanning himself with a dirty old hat. Trina was busy embroidering a black collar with black designs for a new dress for the girl. Night fell, and Trina put the birthday girl to bed and asked the nanny to sleep with her. The mother made herself comfortable in the next room while the poet opted to sleep in one of the stables. He liked the bad smells. There, he hung up a dirty hammock, and under the pretext of being indisposed, he drank some of Candelaria's tea that made him sleep so well. *I hope tomorrow the surprise goes well; I have spent a potosí*, was his last thought. Chano arrived secretly at dawn, liking to ride on a platform "without a frock coat." When he arrived, it was so dark that he tripped over a chair and fell face-first against the showcase, breaking some dishes. The scandal was such that everyone in the house woke up. Trina was helping Chano when the nanny came running in, screaming.

"Don't make such a fuss. I had a hard time putting the little girl to sleep. She is excited about her cake... if only she knew the big surprise that awaits her."

At six o'clock in the morning, Dadhá woke up and found his presents, but curiously, they all had their wrappings open. She didn't think much of it and began to play with them. After half an hour, her mother came in to congratulate her and dress her for breakfast and cake.

After the morning feast, during which the girl ate two pieces of "*brazo de reina*" with lots of tomatoes and a big slice of chocolate cake, she was invited to go out. To her surprise, when she opened the door, she found all the inhabitants of the hacienda dressed up to celebrate her birthday with a "*vaquería*[4]."

And the dances began. The one called *Torito* made her laugh because the women would run around chasing the men with horns in hand, who would give them a few passes until the dancer stumbled and went to the ground. But the ribbon dance caught her attention the most: tied to a large pole with a small hat at the end, a dozen multicolored strips fell to the floor. The dancers picked them up and began to dance, intertwining them

---

[4] Popular peasant dance, typical of Yucatán.

to the pole. Suddenly, her sight stopped at the top of the pole, and sharpening her eyes, she thought she saw some tiny beings with pointed ears, about thirty centimeters long, dancing to the rhythm of the jarana. She got a little closer and confirmed that they were two little men. She had just met the aluxes. In an instant, they jumped, and for a while, she did not see them again. The girl, pleasantly impressed, enjoyed the spectacle in her honor until the two little men tugged at her dress to make her bend down. They whispered something to her, and she nodded. Before long, the girl slipped away from her party.

The emergency bell rang until about fifty workers and their wives gathered on the steps. Trina gave out orders to search for her, and the farm manager divided the search party into four groups. As it was getting dark, they lit their torches and headed into the bush. They searched all night but found nothing. Late in the afternoon of the next day, a farmer returning from working the henequen told them that he thought he had heard the little girl's voice coming from the big cenote, but he could not see her. In droves, the workers ran there with Trina in front. They arrived, and yes, they heard Dadhá's little voice singing and laughing. But the descent was very difficult; there were no stairs, only some tree roots hanging down to the water mirror. It was Brígido, who had heard the bells and joined the search, the first one who, without hesitation, grabbed a vine and descended to the crystal clear and wonderful water. He swam to a small shore, and from there, he saw Dadhá on a small ledge, playing with some clay figurines and laughing alone as if she were with other children.

"Girl, girl, how did you get there?" he asked.

She pointed into a small cavern. "Don't move, let me see how I get there," he told her.

"Nooo, I'm coming!" she replied, standing up and getting lost in the caves' recesses as if nothing had happened. In a couple of minutes, she appeared behind the crowd. She gave no explanation until late at night when she told her mother.

"Mom, don't close the window; Chel needs to get out and come back again."

"Chel? Who is Chel?"

"The little boy in front of you."

After being interrogated, Dadhá explained to her mother that during her party, Chel, a small, short, chubby "goblin-boy" dressed in a turquoise camisole, necklace, little huaraches, and straw hat, invited her to play with his little siblings. she confessed to her mother that she had gone into the kitchen and, without anyone noticing, had taken some oranges and put them in a *sabucán*[5]. And she left with Chel.

"They," she said to her mother, who was growing paler and paler by the second, "live there and have a secret entrance. We played, ate, rafted, and they taught me to sign. I talked and talked, and they sang. There, where there is a rainbow that spins, lives the whole family; they are all little like Chel. They have magical animals: a little flying pig, a margay, a pheasant with arrows in its tail, and a big two-headed black iguana. The canoes have eyes, and a colorful snake with feathers takes care of them. It was a lot of fun," she assured her with a smile. "But I'm sleepy now," and without further ado, she slept all day. That night, Trina slept in slumber with the windows closed, the nanny on the floor under the child's hammock, and the candles burning. She prayed until, in the early morning, she fell asleep.

When she awoke, she found Dadhá sitting on the floor, playing with what she deduced was an imaginary friend. The cook,

---

[5] Bag made of sisal or other vegetable fiber.

Josefina, told her that she had been told about the aluxes. She explained their appearance and told her that not everyone could see them. Trina smiled dismissively and ordered the young girl to take a bath and went to have breakfast. In the dining room, Juanra was eating as if nothing had happened. Trina was indignant at his indifference and proceeded to tell him about the aluxes and what had happened. The man took a sip of coffee and only said.

"Now it turns out that my daughter is crazy."

After spending the weekend as inseparable friends, Dadhá told Chel.

"Come live with me in Mérida; I spend my time alone. The only ones who pay attention to me are the girls, and that's out of obligation. My mom is always embroidering and telling me to study and listen to my dad, you know, the screamer, but sometimes I want to talk to someone. Just because I'm six years old doesn't mean I should keep my thoughts to myself," her friend, moved by her words, told her.

"When you were born, I was born. On the same day. We are the same, although you are very big and everybody can see you. I'd love to come with you, let me tell my mom, and if she gives me permission I'll be on the platform on time," he jumped out the window and got lost in the bush.

It was hot, it was almost noon, and they would leave after lunch to avoid, if possible, traveling at night. Chel knew this, and in a few minutes, he was entering his underworld through the usual door behind the big stone with scribbles on it.

He descended a soft path of bioluminescent moss, felt the humidity, and said, "I'm really going to miss this smell." He reached the village, which, to the layman's eye, amidst the mist, was a row of medium-sized stones arranged whimsically. His eyes were filled with turquoise lights as it became clearer. In the middle of the small esplanade, the light decomposed as it passed through the humidity and painted the stones in colors, transforming them into little houses (otoxes) filled with moss, small plants, and some exotic flowers. Between stone and stone, precious hammocks of different colored threads were hung, and the members of his community rested in them. They had a small shelter on one side, carved in a way that allowed the alux to hide from danger and shielded them from the cool of the night and the animals.

He arrived with his mother, Doña Matush, who, sitting in her hammock, asked him where he was. He told her about his desire to go to Mérida with Dadhá, and she just smiled. There was nothing that was not allowed. Their customs were simple: they were free and only ate fruits and vegetables. Their diet, totally vegan, was easy to obtain because of the natural richness of the environment. They were terrified of cockroaches and scorpions for being evil beings of the night and because they could get sick with their bite or sting.

Doña Matush raised her hand, and in a minute, her whole family surrounded her.

"Chel tells me he is going to Mérida."

His brother, Purutz, said he wanted to go with him, but his mother told him.

"You are like a second self to Chel. You hear his thoughts, feel what happens to him, and perceive what he sees. The same goes for him. He needs to know how we are and we need to know how he is, in case there is something important he needs to be aware of. So, I need you to stay with us." Purutz lowered his head, and small tears welled up in his eyes in the form of big golden drops that became part of the mist and the rainbow. Chel hugged him, reminding him how much he loved him and that physical distance is nothing when you live within each other.

"Remember, son, beware of cockroaches. Eat well, don't get into mischief, and don't let them see you; stay away from the rice powder that gives us away. Think of us, and we will think of you. Then everything will be all right," concluded Mrs. Matush.

The little colorful margay wagged its tail and grunted sadly as its little friend took his sack with his things and got lost on the colorful trail. When Chel came out into the open air, he felt uneasy and climbed a large Ceibo tree to see the hacienda. He realized they were already leaving, a little ahead of schedule, and cut through the henequen stalks to where they would be passing. However, they were already far away; he would not make it. On the verge of giving up, he saw his friend, the rabbit Tontón, and asked him to take him with his vertiginous speed. With a unique fur full of tiny golden crosses, the animal flew with the little creature on his back until he intercepted the platform.

Minutes before, Dadhá was the last one to get in. She was anxious because her little friend had not arrived, and her father scolded her for taking time pretending she had diarrhea and had to go to the bathroom. With one hand, he grabbed her by the ear and forced her onto the platform, which immediately, pulled by a strong mule, took off. The girl cried until, a few miles away from a stone in the hillside, Chel's figure emerged, who, with a long jump, fell on his friend's legs. She explained that she couldn't stop their departure and complained about the ear-pulling. Without wasting any time, the alux jumped over the two benches, came face to face with Juanra, who could not see him and gave him a loud slap. The bewildered father only managed to scream and wonder what had happened. Dadhá, on the other hand, burst out laughing.

From a very young age, when she heard rain, Dadhá would fall asleep, imagining the rain she did not yet know, talking with her little companion. One night, she asked him why she was the only one who could see them, and he told her.

"Humans only see what they want to see. Today, when we went to mass, your Aunt Candita didn't look at anyone. Many greeted her, but she did not see them because she was not interested in seeing them. Human beings see exclusively what they somehow need: they perceive a deer, a rabbit, or a turkey in the distance because they are hunting it for food. Like today, many little angels were flying over your head during mass, and you didn't see or hear them singing beautifully. You wanted friends without caring if they were rich or poor, pretty or ugly, just equals to play with, without judging, and you were ready to see us. That's why you see us. That's all there is to it. At the next mass, raise your eyes, and you'll see the angels watching over us. Mind you, they are not like I imagined. They are very beautiful but different."

The following day, after breakfast and after much thought, Dadhá walked down the dark hallway of her house to the room of her father, Juanra. She found him writing in a corner on his rickety bedside table, hunched over and saw him thinner than usual.

"Dad, I need to talk to you," to which the curmudgeon argued.

"I'm working, can't you see?" He stared at the ceiling, making an effort to control himself. His jaw was trembling with anger.

Dadhá realized it but took a deep breath and began recounting how she met Chel, Purutz, their family, and their margay.

"They're real, Dad," she told him vehemently. She told him of their village, the secret door, and a trip to the X'lacah cenote, navigating the subway rivers in small live rafts with a stone house full of old clay dolls. She said, "Look here," giving him an ancient book of archaeological ruins engravings and showing him a picture of Dzibichaltún and its cenote. Juanra took the book, looked at it with contempt and a little surprise, and said to her.

"You must have dreamed it, and you must have seen this book before; it's your imagination, it's not reality."

"And what is the reality?" asked the girl.

"Well, which one is it going to be? This one!" the grumpy man replied, opening his arms and pointing at his surroundings. "Every morning," he added, "I wake up with rheumatism, and when I open my eyes, I'm sore, and I don't want to know anything about writing, but I have to do it, or else we won't eat. Now go to your room! Don't take up my time; I have to finish this love poem for the children."

The girl went out crying while Chel, who witnessed everything, gave her an invisible "you'll see" sign. Juanra thought, *These orders, I only do them for money and because it is for the priest Ávila, a very good friend of Candelaria. He shook his head negatively to ask himself, where will Dadhaita get these crazy things from? Now, she has strange visions. Just what I needed!* and shook his head as if trying to forget what he had heard.

That evening, it rained. Juanra's screams could be heard all over the house, grumbling about his rheumatism and ordering Dadhá to be locked up in her room. She went to sleep early, wrapped up in a flannel nightgown and wool socks because of the humidity. She did not protest the heat, preferring to wait for the maid to come out of her room to free her legs from the torment of itching. That night, they didn't hang her hammock and instead forced her to sleep in her bed. Chel kept her company, but he was angry that she had been made to cry. He went to confront Juanra for doubting his existence, which he considered an insult. The little girl, meanwhile, sweated like sick because it was so hot that she could not sleep, but when she did, she returned to her recurring dream: a house surrounded by jungle, cenotes, and elves who sang to her and told her wonderful things.

For his part, the alux slipped out of the girl's room, crouched inside the room of the older man who had disturbed her, and waited. As usual, Juan Rafael Medici, whom everyone called Juanra, drank four teas before going to sleep, and just before falling asleep, he got up again to take out the chamber pot to urinate. It was at that moment that he began to discharge his bladder. The little creature silently dragged the pot. Rafael began to follow it, a little frightened, all over the room, wetting his feet and peeing everywhere, all over the sloppy floor. Terrified, he climbed into bed without drying his feet.

Chel got used to sleeping in his friend's bed. He liked to tell her extraordinary things and kept revealing unimaginable secrets. For example, that the dead only changed bodies. They leave behind all of their earthly possessions in their corpse, and instead, the good qualities of each person are reincarnated in an animal, usually a rabbit or squirrel. If someone had a white soul, they would be reincarnated in an Alux, whereas someone with a black soul would be reincarnated in a cockroach or scorpion. The worst ones were those who asked forgiveness from their gods before dying without being repentant and cynically demanded to get to heaven. They were reincarnated as vultures. They would fly but eat rotten meat until they died and would be reborn repeatedly as scavenger animals.

The bodies were something else. It was the souls that received punishment. Bodies already without souls were as innocent as newborns, inspired peace, and kept all the pure things we bring from birth.

Dadhá, therefore, developed a strange fascination with "those earthly things," the bodies that the dead left behind. They transmitted peace to her.

"Why do you call yourself that?" Dadhá asked her friend.

"For the place where I was born. Do you remember I took you to the doll's house when we met? Well, the cenote where we arrived is called X'lacah, and that's why they named me X'lá, but they call me Chel because of my light hair and skin. They say I was born from an old soul. X'lacah means old town. I guess that's why."

4

The noise was imperceptible to everyone except for Chel. It was like footsteps and murmurs. It certainly wasn't an animal. *Animals can't open doors or windows, he thought.* Without wasting any time, he climbed into the black hammock with tassels and canopy where Dadhá was sleeping, with that restless sleep that characterized her.

They had arrived the night before. It would be the seventh birthday of the girl, who, on this occasion, had little trouble convincing her father, Juanra, to spend her birthday at her uncle Chano's hacienda. This time, Dadhá showed up at her father's office who was picking his ugly nose, reading the newspaper and raging as he looked through the paper because there was not a single review of the book *Secretos de Palacio* (*Palace Secrets*) about Governor Carrillo Puerto's alleged dalliances and his penchant for having fun, especially with foreign women. Among what the writer revealed was that the lyrics of "Peregrina" (Traveler), written by Luis Rosado Vega and sung by Ricardo Palmerín, included some revealing verses:

"When you leave
my palm trees and my land,
traveler
with your charming demeanor,

don't forget,
don't forget about my land,
don't forget,
don't forget about my love."

He claimed in his book, of which one hundred copies had been published and only two had been sold, Don Felipe had fallen in love with the American journalist Alma Reed, correspondent and special envoy of the *New York Times* to the city of Mérida at the height of the pandemic. He did not respect the tragedy of the hundreds of deaths caused by the disease and spent all his time with the gringa! He deserved to be executed, but we still need to know the dreary stories that took place in the Palace!

"Those corrupt journalists!" he howled like a wounded animal. "They haven't written a word about my book! I sent them a copy a month ago, and they haven't written a single word about me!"

Advised by her friend, Dadhá stood up in front of her father and said.

"I know how to get everything you want published tomorrow."

Juanra was about to start questioning her, and she raised her hand while her accomplice be-gan to move the books, which impressed the curmudgeon because he swore his daughter had mystic powers.

"No, don't tell me anything. Let's make a deal," she told him. "You write something about your book, give it to me, and tomo-rrow, you can read it on the front page. If it is published, you take me to spend my seventh birthday at my uncle's hacienda for two weeks. If nothing happens, you won't celebrate my birthday, not even with a cake."

Faced with such an offer, in which he could save the cost of the party and the "heavy expense of the cake," he replied.

"All right, I'll write the review of my great work, but if you're pulling my leg, not only will we not go to the hacienda, but you won't go out in the yard to play for a month, and you won't eat dessert. Understood? Now get out; I don't like the smell of a clean girl."

Soon, Chel was running through the city streets on his way to the newspaper with the review in his hands. Although the alux was invisible, the sheets of paper were not, so he had to sneak along the road when carrying something material, such as the self-congratulatory writ-ing. It was easy for him to find the buil-ding. Before leaving, he sniffed the previous day's newspaper for a few minutes and detected the strong smell of lead from the ink. As he stepped out into the street, he raised his head and waited to perceive where that particular scent was coming from.

When he arrived, he searched for the editors' office for several minutes. He guessed who they were because they operated the same machines as Dadhá's father. At the back of the large room, where half a dozen people were huddled together typing, an older man was strok-ing his gray hair with a desperate look. He was, coincidentally, the newspaper chronicler who had been attacked by the blank page syndrome. He had not written a line for two weeks and had already been asked by the editor to write "some-thing, and preferably something funny."

The alux waited for a tummy ache because he had eaten beans for breakfast, and when he finally had it, he jumped on the older man's messy desk and threw a blue kiis with which, immediately, the famous Renato Alarcón y Ceballos, along with the entire edi-torial staff, fell into a brief and unusual sleep. Chel approached his ear, told him the story, and placed the writing on the typewriter. Before the man woke up, the alux repeated that he, as the great chronicler he was, had written such a review and had to present it without fail to the director, who would say yes. Chel planned to speak in his ear. As he did not wake up, he slapped him until the older man found himself with red cheeks and the writing in front of him. The crea-ture did the same with the director, and in a couple of jumps, he was on the street. Without the bulky letter in his hands, he closed his eyes and oriented himself, and in seconds, he was with Dadhá, to whom she only said.

"Don't worry, pretty; vanity is a powerful thing, mission accomplished, tomorrow you will have your permission."

"Dadhá, ninia, someone is invading our farm. Wake up!"

With a jump, the little girl sat up in bed and stared bewildered at the little alux.

"What's wrong?"

"I hear noises with my lower ears, and they are from some uninvited alux. Come with me to see who they are," he hurried, "Grab a stick from the pavilion so we can protect us, they may be Bavarian gnomes who like meat and are very grumpy."

"Let's see," the girl asked her little companion, "what is this Bavarian gnome?"

The alux looked at her impatiently and explained that there was no time to waste.

"Oh, I'll explain later."

Dadhá did not give in; she frowned, twisted her mouth, and stood firm.

"Tell me now!"

Impatient, Chel explained to her in broad terms that in Xibalbá inhabited aluxes but also other goblins from all over the world, who had arrived with their masters in the merchant ships. When they died, the long-lived goblins had found shelter in the caves of the Maya under-world.

"And that's it!" said the alux. I'll tell you more later; now, let's move, or they'll steal every-thing!"

And indeed, when they peeked into the kitchen, they found a curious scene: four little red-haired goblins dressed in bright colors. The alux recognized them and said to Dadhá, relieved.

"No, they are not the Germans. They are my friends, the Mazzamurellis."

"Giovani, Giancarlo! What are you doing stealing from us?"

"Chel, my friend," said Giovani, "we didn't want to wake you up, and yesterday we looked for you, but you hadn't arrived from Mérida. Today is Grandma Antoniella's birthday, she is one hundred and thirty years old, and she wants to eat pasta. Since you haven't been here for months and yesterday afternoon we saw you arrive, we thought you could donate us a little flour and some tomatoes. We were thinking of inviting you and your family, but we were going to wait for you to wake up. Look," he said pitifully, "because of the rains, we have been having a hard time. Don Kauil gave us some mushrooms a few days ago, and that's what we've been surviving on, but today is a holiday."

Dadhá, who had been merely observing, intervened.

"You can take whatever you want; no one would notice here. What's more, I'll help you, and when the sun rises, I'll ask Doña Josefina to make me a tamarind cake, and I'll take it to you... if you invite me."

And the joy spread. The mazzamurellis began to dance following an Italian rhythm while the girl filled a small bag with provisions: flour, an egg, a large tomato ball, Parmesan cheese, salt, and garlic. She also put them a loaf of French bread and a bundle of spinach.

"What time is the party?" she asked amused.

"When you want it to start *Principessa*, we will dance and sing all day; it is a happy date, and making Neapolitan Capellini for all the guests will take time.

Loaded with their provisions, the multicolored beings disappeared into the darkness of the mountain. Their songs could be heard in the distance. They were happy with very little.

Chel explained to his friend.

This is what life is all about: being happy making others happy, especially older adults who should be doubly happy. One thing I can tell you, *ninia*, is that they are grateful like all noble souls. When you need something the most, do not doubt that a poor alux like me, or even poorer like Giovani, we will be ready to help you as you are helping now. With your kindness, you filled those who had nothing with joy, and now they are happier because they have you.

After breakfast, Dadhá asked permission to go and spend the day at Doña Petronila's house with her daughter Silvia, to which her mother said no. In an instant, she turned to her father, made a secret signal to her little friend to make a mess, and raised her arms as the table moved. Not slow or lazy, Juanrá said to Trina.

"Let her go; let her stay and eat over there, don't contradict her."

Upon entering the Xibal village, the pheasant recognized the girl in black who, together with her inseparable friend, arrived laden with things to eat, mainly fruit. They gave a slice of tangerine to the beautiful custodian, who shook his fearsome feathers in thanks and flanked them.

As soon as they arrived, the villagers gathered around them to embrace them, all except the shy Cuxo, who had not been able to fly that day because he was more chubby than ever. Dadhá fetched him and carried him lovingly. In the distance, Don Kauil's voice could be heard ordering them to get into the canoes, which were ready. They all climbed in military order, and Dadhá and Chel were given the biggest one for themselves.

"Look," he told her after a short time sailing in turquoise waters. "That village belongs to my cousins. They are getting ready for the feast, as they have many children and are very poor. They don't take care of the corn and always suffer hardships. Today, they are going to get purple from eating so much."

A little further on, they came to a place full of flowers. It was the most arranged place of the Xibal.

"Here," he said, "live two charming aluxes: Jeromín, the breadwinner, and Cirilo, who likes to be called "la china" and is the one who cleans the otox. They live with the mother of Cirilo because the latter does not know how to eat alone and refuses to let Jeromín feed him in his mouth, as his mother, Doña Chabela, who is known as a gossiper and a troublemaker, does. They, eternal sweethearts, are in charge of weaving hammocks with scraps of thread and sisal that they collect. They are getting ready for the party; they are so cute."

As they rounded the bend next to a large stalactite that sparkled with its millions of tiny crystals, they encountered the village of the Spaniards, who were also summoned and greeted them warmly. In the distance, Chel stood watching in amusement the little Spanish girls, Andalusians who liked to dance Sevillanas all the time. In that village, everyone worked to eat well and made sure there was enough bread and gazpacho.

Arriving at a fork, Chel told her.

"Look, here we have to decide: if we follow the short way, we pass through the village of the Germans, who are sometimes aggressive and may even try to approach you to rob you. But the long way, you go through a dark area, where you can find cockroaches, and they will realize that the village is empty and could invade it. I think my grandfather will know how to decide." And he hadn't finished saying that when they took the road that went through the Germanic village.

A few minutes later, the caravan stopped, and Don Kauil jumped down and began to converse with what Dadhá thought was a strange being. It was a Germanic gnome, greenish in color, who had crossed a log over the subway river.

They negotiated for a few minutes, and finally, the older alux gave them a sack of corn, and the gnomes let them pass. The youngest of them, way at the end of the passage, leaned over a ledge and sent a thunderous kiss to Dadhá to the cry of *"Hübsches Mädchen."* Without understanding the language, she smiled and blushed. All women have always known when they are called pretty.

Suddenly, they arrived at an enchanted valley. The sun penetrated through a large hole atop a "mul," an ancient Mayan shrine, where the grass grew green from so much rain. On the edges of the valley, a kind of sea grapes grew, which provided the Mazzamurellis with enough raw material to make a sweet wine that they drank on happy days and exchanged for corn with other villages when the harvest was good.

Upon seeing them, Giovani approached and began shouting in Italian.

"É arrivata la piccola bambina che vive nella fattoria, si chiama Dadhá."

And the party began. The canoe breathed a sigh of relief when the girl got off, as she was too big for it. Cuxo did his best and flew two meters before the applause of the mazzamurellis, who, surprised, jumped with emotion. That day, the girl learned to cook the best of sauces and danced and sang, to exhaustion, melodies that she did not know but that, in the end, she learned from singing them so much, especially one that said:

*"La donna è mobile
Qual piuma al vento
Muta d'accento
E di pensiero"*

In a quiet moment, she looked at a large bed of yellow flowers surrounded by colorful pebbles.

"What is that?" she asked Chel.

Giovanni stepped forward and said in Spanish with an Italian accent.

"Today, a new being must come to us. Let me explain: we, the aluxes, are always conceived at full moon. Giancarlo's older brother, Massimo, married last full moon, and his partner has been waiting since then. We aluxes take a long time to arrive from one moon to another, and the time has come. The baby will be born as soon as the moon comes out."

And so it was said and done. Within minutes, the early moon caused a commotion among the mazzamurellis, and Vitoria, the pregnant goblin, was carried to the yellow bed.

It was Massimo who lit the fire and stood next to her, who, in a quick movement, lifted up her camisole to expose her belly. Suddenly, as the first rays of moonlight entered through the rocks, a multicolored bubble began to sprout magically from Vittoria's navel and grew bigger and bigger. The colors changed until two remained: gold and turquoise. Everyone shouted: "It will be a *bambina*, it will be a *bambina*!" Dadhá asked why, to which several said in chorus.

"If it had been gold and amber, it would have been a bambino."

And indeed, without warning, the large two-colored sphere burst like a soap bubble and, from the center, fell into the hands of the new father, a beautiful little elf. As if it had been practiced, all the elves shouted in unison the name that had been revealed to them up to that moment: Patriccia! And they sang again:

"La donna è mobile
Qual piuma al vento
Muta d'accento
E di pensiero"

There were hugs and dances, and when the grape juice began to flow, it began to get dark. Dadhá said goodbye, and when she left, she promised to return every year to celebrate Doña Antoniella and Patriccia. The matriarch kissed her and, in passing, laughed a lot, but affectionately, at the black dress of her guest and said to her.

"Tomorrow is pilgrimage day to the Great Xibal. Come with us; Kukul will make his debut. It will be wonderful."

Dadhá had no problems with her parents, telling them she played dolls all day with her friend Silvia. Trina did not protest, and Juanrá told her relieved.

"It was a quiet day, without noise; if you want, you can return tomorrow and bring them the meal's leftovers. 'We must not waste the nach stew.' "

When they arrived very early at the Xibal, Don Kauil welcomed them, but not before arguing with Don Dzoc, Chel's father, because he had not moved from the hammock for days and had not grown mushrooms to eat. The older alux shouted at him to get up and, at the same time, kicked the hammock, which, with the blow, turned 180 degrees, and Dzoc fell face-first on his old mat. Don Kauil hurried him to harvest ten baskets of mushrooms and ten baskets of tender corncobs for the trip and pushed him, with the help of his staff, to the fields. He sentenced him to stay and look after the village with the margay Xumi, four pheasants, and the three aluxes that had worked the least lately. They would have to be vigilant and eat frugally to avoid falling asleep.

When he saw Dadhá, the old alux shouted joyfully, and Doña Matush ran out to greet them. In front came her grandson with a big bag of vegetables and a gigantic pot of kabax beans.

"Now we are ready; get in line to board, we are going to the Great Xibal!" Don Kauil shouted loudly.

As on the previous day, the aluxes sailed placidly along the turquoise river until they reached the fork. On this occasion, Don Kauil said to them very seriously.

"Today, we will go through the dark area because the 'Chan mozón' will take us to our desti-nation just past it. Light the fire and incense burners to scare away the insects!"

All of the aluxes already knew what to do. Xumi became alert, and the pheasants, strategically placed at the tips of the canoes, spread their feathers and began to shake them as dozens of tor-ches broke the darkness. At first, they saw nothing strange, but hundreds of red eyes stalked them as they went deeper. Don Kauil reassured them.

"They will not attack us because we are prepared, and they see us strong. They attack the weak and distracted. Wave the torches, and nothing will happen. Let's sing; insects hate joy."

And so, moving the torches and singing a melody that Dadhá taught them, they passed with-out consequence among the inha-bitants of the dark zone:

"Purutzón Cahuich, nacido en Tahmek,
un pobre huinic, con cara de pec

que siendo un dziritz su papa don Dzoc
lo dejó colís de tanto huascop[6]*"*

The light returned, and the journey continued placidly through the glimmers of light on the river. Dadhá asked.

"How much longer?" to which Chel said.

"If we were sailing down the river, it would take weeks, but we are already arriving at Chan Mozón; it will be a matter of a little while."

"And what is that?" asked the girl when she spotted a large, colorful swirl on the stream.

"That's the Mozón that will take us to Xibal," said her companion. "Are you dizzy?" he asked just before starting to turn.

One by one, the canoes entered the big foamy hole until it was the turn of Dadhá and Chel's cheem.

She never knew for sure how much time passed. In fact, curiously enough, it was both fast and slow. At first, the raft was spinning towards the center of the water walls and falling into the void, but as the void swallowed them, the canoe stabilized, and suddenly, instead of going down, they began to move horizontally at great speed. It was as if the whirlpool had become a gigantic tunnel that carried them smoothly. The aluxes sang their songs, and suddenly, they began to ascend. When they reached the mouth of the Mozón, they began to turn again, and it was the water and its constant movement that expelled them from its center.

Everything was foggy. There was a relative darkness and a peculiar smell, like wet stone, moss, and market. When it cleared up, Dadhá was surprised: they were in the middle of a majestic

---

[6] A popular song in Yucatán. It can translate as: The fat Cahuich, born in Tahmek, a poor dog-faced man who as a little boy was left bald by his father Don Dzoc from so many knocks on his head.

turquoise-colored cenote surrounded by an immense construction with four triangular walls leaning towards the center. And at the top, a kind of small window let in light. Without understanding what it was about, she looked more closely and realized that all around the cenote, there were many tiny stone houses. And before her was revealed a very active and bustling little metropolis. The cheem approached the cenote's edge, bordered by a stone path up to what looked like a marketplace, and disembarked.

"We have arrived," said Don Kauil with a tone of triumph. Let's stick together so that no one gets lost, but if it happens, come to the cheem before nightfall.

Chel and Dadhá, always together, did not cease to be surprised at every step. The place was a mixture of beings from all over the world. There was a zone for each nationality, but the Aztec Chaneques predominated, competing with the Mayan Aluxes in population. The Chaneques, unlike the Aluxes, were taller by about ten centimeters and spoke in a singsong voice, but they greeted politely. After a few steps, they encountered hundreds of aluxes and various goblins trading with each other on the edge of the cenote. Don Kauil stopped at a stall full of multicolored flowers and exchanged half a basket of mushrooms for a canoe full of yellow, red, orange, and violet flowers.

"They are all edible," explained Chel. They are from around here, and the chaneques collect them.

Also, the *tatich* bought half a canoe of coconuts in exchange for the other half a basket of mushrooms. The hours went by, and the expedition leader did not tire of exchanging mushrooms and corn for the most varied vegetables and aromatic plants from stall to stall.

Finally, they left the market area and walked along the edge of the cenote among screaming mazzamurellis announcing their little trattoria and the delicacies they prepared; Chinese elves, offering bread; Germans, showing their sausages; Spaniards, selling fish shouting, "*Tenemos pez dama blanca, pez ciego, hay filete de carpa!*" while the Spaniard girls were giving flamenco dance lessons, but the aluxes passed by because in the rainbow village, everyone, even little Cuxo, was a vegetarian.

Around noon, the immense enclosure was filled with light. In the first row, close to the cenote, were the merchants. But a little further back, hundreds, thousands of small stone houses crowded together to form a large city with its small streets. What most fascinated Dadhá were the colorful stores that filled what she understood as a second row. Restaurants, trinket stores, stalls of various stones such as quartz and lapis lazuli, new torches, necklaces, tin dishes, wooden Kimbomba sets, oils, achiote in grain and ground, essences and various condiments, and everything else one could imagine.

Don Kauil decided to eat at the Indian goblins' place since he loved curry. He sat down with all the inhabitants of Xibal and ordered each of their favorite dishes from memory. Only when he reached Dadhá did he stop, "And for the girl... for the girl..."

"What are you eating, pretty girl?"

She laughed and told him she would eat the same as him. There was total excitement, and they only talked about the descent of Kukulkán, which that year would be in the early afternoon, and the annual game of Kimbomba. Suddenly, from one end of the great Xibal came the voice of Memux, the master of ceremonies, telling the debutants to get ready. Kukul got ready instantly and went to meet his peers who would descend with the light of Kukulkán from the external part of the portentous construction: the pyramid of Chichén Itzá. When finished, all would have the power to fertilize the earth with their presence alone. And Memux shouted again.

"After the event, we will celebrate the traditional Kimbomba game in honor of the graduates. Go out the west end; the gate is already open, and the jaguars and pheasants guard the area! There is no danger. The sky is clear, and Kukulkán will descend!"

The aluxes and other goblins happily trooped towards the exit and settled on one side of the pyramid. For his part, Kukul crawled up an inner staircase that passed by a chamber where a stone jaguar with beautiful jade eyes was kept. At the top of the pyramid, the debutants prepared for the arrival of the great magical serpent. They did not have to wait long. Suddenly, the sunlight began forming triangular shadows projected on the main staircase, creating a pattern in the form of a snake. With the light, dozens of the small reptiles, along with Kukul, were slowly descending in a mesmerizing choreography.

It was a magical moment. The aluxes danced celebrating that that year, Kukulkán had been more luminous than ever, so they would have a great harvest. In the distance, among the jungle, the workers in charge of the pyramid reconstruction rested without noticing the fantastic event. Arriving at the base, Kukul was greeted by the entire village gathered there to dance to old Mayan and Aztec melodies.

Memux's voice was heard from the top of the great pyramid.

"Everyone to the Kimbomba game!"

Don Kauil, as "*tatich*" of Xibal, had a special place among his peers. The others settled along the immense field whose high walls were highlighted by four stone hoops. Chel explained to Dadhá that when the Maya humans inhabited the area, they played with a rubber ball that was too heavy for them. Over the centuries, their ancestors adapted it and played circular Kimbomba.

"What is that?" she asked, and Chel proudly explained.

"There are many players, and everyone will have a chance. The objective of this game is to hit the joroch, a sacred wood of chacá, with a medium-sized stick called che', which is made of sapote wood. The joroch must jump, and when it reaches their waist height, they must hit it forcefully to make it fly. It is not a common wood," he continued, "it is thousands of years old, and only on this day, at this hour, the joroch gains strength thanks to the descent of Kukulkán, and if they hit it well, it will fly through the four rings and return to the player's hands. The first one to achieve it will win the honor of guarding it until the next descent of Kukulkán.

Finally, after a hundred young men tried, an alux from Cobá, Codzito, about fifteen years old, gave a perfect blow. The joroch rose about a meter, and Codzito hit it with his che' a tremendous blow that was heard all over Chichén, and the joroch flew off to pass, spinning vertiginously on its own axis, through the four rings in a magical flight. Codzito, as was tradition, closed his eyes and extended his hand. The joroch, after its perambulation, landed gently on it. And the enthusiasm overflowed. "The joroch lives, the joroch lives!" "Bravo, Codzito!" The aluxes invaded the court and carried the Kimbomba winner all over the field. He was, that day, the hero of Xibalbá.

When the afternoon began to fall, Don Kauil indicated it was time to return, but they would take the long route to navigate a whirlpool that would leave them near Xibal. He would take advantage of the occasion to buy some jade eyes from the Arabian goblins who were on their way, as he had to make initiation necklaces for three aluxes who had reached six years of age.

As they rounded a bend, they were overtaken by two shining cheems resembling gold, and the crew members were dressed in white with their turban of the same color. They were the leaders of the village's inhabitants founded by goblins who came with some traders from the Middle East some decades ago.

Suddenly and when the luxury canoe left them behind, Dadhá had to rub her eyes; on the highest part of a rock, a small camel with big pointed ears, with many colors and three humps, was guarding the entrance to the area.

The little girl burst out laughing and infected all the crew members of the cheems that, like a little train, were bound in line with each other.

Arriving at an immense cenote with steep walls, a towering dome, and an uninhabitable view, she was enraptured by an artificial formation in the shape of a palm tree that jutted out of the blue waters and gave a floor to the small tents set up on each "leaf" of the plant.

The *tatich* raised his hand, and his cheem let go of the others to enter one of the canals between two palm-shaped embankments. With a bound, he jumped in front of a tent and began to call out to his friend Jalil.

Dadhá did not lose, amused, detail of the negotiation between Don Kauil and a big-nosed alux dressed in white because it seemed, at times, that they would come to blows because of the shouts they gave each other, and after two minutes, they embraced and laughed. Finally, they agreed on what she calculated would be the price of the jade because Don Kauil took out a bag with black stones and handed them to his friend. "Obsidian," said Chel secretly, "only we have it." In turn, Don Jalil gave him a bag with jade stones, and after a dialogue in a strange language, they said goodbye with the promise to meet in Xibal. Almost as soon as they ar-rived, Dadhá, mischievous, covered the eyes of the Cheem, who did not see a sharp stone and damaged its hull. The water began to flow, and they barely reached the shore while the small raft sank. Everyone came to the rescue of the girl, Chel, and the Cheem, who almost drowned. All the members of the Xibal lowered their heads and turned their backs on Dadhá. They had offered her the best, and she despised it. She would not enter the Xibal for a long time. She had hurt one of their own.

Hours before, when the Xibal caravan passed through the dark and smelly zone on its way to the Great Xibal, the chief cockroach, K'uruchón, devised a plan, seeing that a large part of the village was going on a journey. He summoned his cockroaches to follow the smelly trail of boiled beans to appropriate such a rich delicacy. Finally, and after leaving the dark zone, they arrived in the vicinity of Xibal, a place of abundant food since the aluxes cultivated different kinds of mushrooms, collected fruits, and stored in a large cave the corn that the humans were dropping as they cultivated it.

However, the chief cockroach was afraid because despite having a powerful bite, his followers could not withstand the strength of the Xumi margay nor the retractable feathers of the pheasants who guarded the entrance to the colorful cave at all times; also, the incredible marksmanship of the aluxes, who were capable of hitting a cockroach with their slingshot at a distance of fifty meters. But this time, apparently, there was no danger. K'uruchón noticed that the few caretakers they had left in the village were lethargic, their bellies swollen, totally defenseless.

He gave the order to the K'uruches, who followed him to steal the beans and as much corn as they could since the small aluxes could not defend themselves. It was the best opportunity of their lives.

They quickly entered the village, and as he had anticipated, everyone was asleep, motionless. The opportunists proceeded to loot the large cave; they numbered in the hundreds and finally had the aluxes' food within their reach.

The cockroaches passed in front of Toh and Loc, who had not fallen into lethargy and tried to catch them with their fearsome jaws, but while one tried to capture whoever passed nearby, the other did the same in the opposite direction. They were utterly ineffective in appearance, but in reality, they were custodians of the sacred stones of the village: a giant flint and a bag with a good amount of pyrite, stones used by the aluxes to make fire, thousands of obsidians, a mysterious ancient key and a secret box of Kahuil. At birth, each alux was cut a piece of flint and given a pyrite stick with which they would make fire most of their lives. Toh and Loc were precisely at the entrance to a small cavity they never left because they could not agree on where to walk. And stubborn as anyone, they were excellent custodians of the treasure that allowed the aluxes to illuminate their caves and trade. It was kept secret from adjacent villages, who came to buy stones when, after a rain, the other beings of the Xibalbá had their fire extinguished. They exchanged it for food or various objects.

When the "food thefts" were more confident looting the cave and taking the products among several, they were paralyzed because from each sentinel began to come out a screeching sound like those produced by cicadas. At that moment, a brother of the snake, Kukul, jumped on K'uruchón and hugged him tightly, breaking some of his legs.

The high-pitched noise announced the inevitable. The first to release a blue *kiis* was Dzoc, who was the most inflated because, besides eating beans, he had eaten a large piece of green mango. Within two seconds, everyone began to fart, and the cave filled with a bluish gas, which left the k'uruches unconscious. As the stinking, drowsy gas was released, the inhabitants woke up from their lethargy and realized hundreds of the foul critters surrounded them passed out upside down. The custodians proceeded to tie up the thieves.

Memux, upon arrival, proposed an exemplary punishment for which he consulted with Don Kauil, the patriarch, about the punishment for the insects. The older alux, who came down from his cheem laboriously and after coordinating the salvage of the sinking canoe, remained thinking for a few seconds, and after raising his staff of power, he said to them.

"Drench the cockroaches with a lot of orange blossom oil in large quantities so that they will learn their lesson. They hate that smell. Oh, tie two legs to them and call the cheems to take them away, out of the cave, so that these thieves can amuse themselves by getting rid of the ants because they love the taste of orange blossom."

Meanwhile, the recently graduated Kukul dragged K'uruchón, who was also tied up and bathed in oil, to a cheem. At the same time, the inhabitants lay down for the effects of the curry after a roar that sounded like the screeching of a hundred cicadas and more blue kiises that sent them flying through the air.

On the eve of Dadhá's departure to Mérida, the chief cockroach, aided by his two stalwarts, managed to free himself from his bonds and make it to the platform where the Médici family would depart for the city. They, in hiding, would also go to finish off Chel. At least, that's what they believed when they got on and concealed themselves in a bale of henequen fibers... that would leave for Europe first thing in the morning.

5

During the Spanish flu pandemic, the Marmite Club, or Marmiton Club, as the smug ones called it, went into recess. The custom of meeting under the pretext of "dealing with transcendent matters," such as, for example, financing protests against the socialist government, demanding the governor to close the ports—the only thing they achieved—or requesting the authorities to pave this or that street, was only a pretext to eat.

Years ago, a beautiful and robust woman arrived in the pilot's boat of the Cavaleiro company from Galicia with two small daughters. All their luggage consisted of a trunk and a large pot, which she called Marmité. Martina García Piñeiro, a cook like few others, soon became known for preparing international but mainly Spanish and Galician food for more than ten people gatherings. Chano's group of friends hired her to prepare abundant food for them on the first Saturday of every month. They were authentic feasts that ended when the bottom of the pots were visible. For twelve gentlemen, another few pounds of food were prepared. They considered it a kind of secret society because of the delicate topics to be discussed, and their meeting point was kept with extraordinary secrecy. Don Huacho Ramos, businessman owner of the only quality pottery and crystal store in Mérida, was in charge of assigning the venue. They met in front of delicious stews uninterruptedly for eight years.

Due to the pandemic, six months had to pass before a singular advertisement was published again in the newspaper *La Carta Peninsular*, which, at that time, caused all kinds of conjectures. In it was a small engraving of the marmite pot, a nickname, and a day.

This time, it was Chano's turn. Thus, the announcement published on Monday called for a meeting of the illustrious assistants of the Sybarite Club on Saturday at Chano's house.

When the man in question saw it, he got worried and went straight to the mirror. He had no hair on his head and no eyebrows. Only his thinning mustache remained. He put on his hat and, determined, headed for Fifty-second Street, where a wig merchant offered a wide variety of models and toupees. He was diligently attended by Don Felipe Gamboa, who immediately invited him to sit on a barber's chair, a job he also did. He served him a Veracruz coffee that he could not resist and took off his hat. The merchant studied him and indicated.

"This has a solution," he went to a display case and pulled out a variety of hairpieces. "They are made of natural hair," he said. "This one is French, good but hot; this one is from Asia, it is cheaper and cooler, but it cannot get wet; and finally, the modern marvel, this one is American, and has a new system, for added security, two small strips of fabric are glued with adhesive and provide resistance against strong winds. The process must be done carefully, wetting it for a long time, because it could harm the scalp. It can be used in the street during the day because it is fresh. It is the most expensive, but it is the one that works best," he said, trying it on his client in front of the big mirror.

As it was a bit long, the wig merchant explained.

"If you like it, you can put it on, and I will trim it to the shape of your face."

Chano smiled and, ignoring the high price, gave the go-ahead. The process, which included shaving the three existing hairs and adjusting the contraption, took a little over an hour. When it was finished, he was satisfied, but he noticed his light eyebrows, and Don Felipe, with a grimace of resignation, gave him only a thick black crayon.

And the day of the feast arrived. Since the night before, Chano had given Candita and Juanra a potent, long-lasting purge so they would not bother during the meal. The problem was that the little girls with whom the Galician woman had arrived a decade before, María Luisa and Mar, had grown into beautiful young women who helped their mother cook and serve the table.

For twelve diners, they prepared a frying pan full of chicharra as a snack, ten good-sized Galician-style octopus, a large paella of saffron rice, two large salt-baked cobias, and as a side dish, fried planiliza roe with handmade tortillas made by the workers of the house. The main course consisted of twelve suckling pigs baked in a wood-fired oven for ten hours, one for each guest. Refried beans in lard and habanero cut garnished the meal. The Galician woman offered chinalima, tamarind, and plum waters for the event. In addition, they set up a dessert table with *tortas de cielo*, custard, almond cake, chocolate truffles, a specialty of one of the daughters who was heartily congratulated by all, and various Yucatecan sweets. The girls were "spoiled" with secret gifts and good tips.

And the feast began. Everyone smiled mockingly at Chano's toupee and his thick eyebrows painted with black crayon. However, he was very proud of his appearance, and at a given moment, precisely when Chel was passing by stealthily to steal some truffles for him and Dadhá, the master of the house took out of a case to show off to his friends, a walking stick with a fluffy rabbit's tail sticking out of its handle. The goblin looked at the object, and he noticed it was lined with white rabbit fur with golden crosses, and a rabbit's foot was attached to the end. Evidently, it belonged to his dear friend Tontón, and this realization filled him with unbridled fury.

Chel jumped up on the table in front of Chano and went up to his head to pull his wig. He had to use all his strength to pull it off with two strips of scalp included, and then he smeared it on his eyebrows. Not satisfied, he hung on to the oily mustache and began to swing on it until he pulled it off. With his mustache in his hands, Chel ran away. The club members did not understand what was happening, and it was when the mustaches left "alone" when the laughter of surprise and mockery broke out. Chano quickly made his escape, and soon after, he left the group of the big gluttons: The Marmiton Club.

6

The days passed quietly. In the silence of the house, which was only broken by Juanra's neurosis, with cries of sorrow and tantrums, one could hear the dripping of the water in the cistern, the creaking of the weather vane, and the singing of the birds. It was Friday, and like every Friday, they would eat a three-meat stew. Dadhá liked it very much, especially because of the ritual she explained to Chel.

"You serve yourself a portion of yellow rice, seasoned with saffron and eat a part. You take from one of the two large plates small portions of seasoned vegetables or meat seasoned in the Yucatecan style: carrot, potato, chayote, corn, cabbage, plantain, and pumpkin from the first one and pork, beef and chicken from the second one. Shred the meat, mash the vegetables with a fork, stir everything together, and from an individual cup, take broth with noodles and spread it over the puch to your liking, as well as onion, radish, habanero pepper, and cilantro. You squeeze a bit of sour orange and accompany the meal with handmade tortillas."

Fridays were like that. On Mondays, beans with pork, and the rest of the week, various stews such as steak casserole, chicken in sweet orange, turkey in black stuffing, papzules, and for dinner, tamalitos, and good bread.

Dadhá, who loved to eat, was brought up to be a princess and, out of nowhere, had begun to speak Italian phrases but had to do everything with style and diligence. That day, and out of sight of everyone, Chel was mischievously sitting on his friend's head criticizing Chano for his baldness and the two colored stripes of the torn-off wig, to which the girl laughed discreetly to the irritation of the adults. The alux began to pull the little girl's cheeks, to open her mouth by pulling her lips, to climb on her head to pull her eyelids before the horror of her parents and uncles, who first looked astonished at the event, turned to see as if to confirm that everyone was witnessing it, and then horrified they only saw how the little girl's face contracted and stretched grotesquely. Her mother's screams were, first, so that she would stop playing on the table, but when they saw her braids rise on their own, they screamed, thinking she was being attacked until Candelaria concluded that it was a possession and began to faint showing her the cross of her long necklace, which unleashed Dadhá's laughter. Chano, frightened, decided that he could drive away the evil forces with water and only managed to take a pitcher of thick horchata with almonds and throw it at her, shouting, "Away evil spirits!" When the liquid fell on the goblin, everyone was aware of his presence as he revealed himself before their eyes, totally white. The meal turned into a riot, and Chano took an old arquebus to attack the underworld being of which his niece spoke so much and whom he suspected had pulled off his toupee and mustache.

Upon seeing the gun, Chel jumped phenomenally and ran down the hallway only to hear two detonations of the weapon, which, fortunately, was loaded with very small ammunition. Candelaria collapsed, fainting in her chair that gave way under her weight, and went backward. Trina and Dadhá shouted at Chano not to shoot, and Juanra hid under the table cowardly. When she heard the detonation, Dadhá threw herself to the floor to protect her friend. The goblin's good fortune meant that he only took two mustard pellets in the butt and uttered an insult in Mayan.

"*Pelaná[7]*, you'll see what happens to you, *uepuchis*; you shot me!"

The latter was heard by everyone present, including the female employees, who laughed because they recognized the voice of an alux.

Dadhá, however, was left lying on the ground. A pellet had penetrated her forehead, and she was unconscious. The girls and Trina, noticing this, carried her to the bed and saw with horror a trickle of blood on the girl's face. Trina screamed.

"Chano, you hurt my daughter!" Juanra simply went to his office, saying, "I'm going to look for some remedy for the wounds," in the middle of the confusion and with his butt hurting, Chel sentenced.

"Chano de porra, there is no room for both of us here, either you leave or I leave... and I think the one who is going to leave is you, cinchado, pelaná!"

The goblin knew that Dadhá was not dead, only wounded, and mentally communicated with Purutz to ask for help. They needed Kauil, who arrived in minutes. Upon hearing of the incident, he forgave Dadhá and extracted the pellet with an ancient Mayan method. They were at peace, and she was named Xibal's favorite daughter. She had saved Chel.

If there was one thing the little alux had, it was the gift of observation from the advantage of invisibility. Thus, he observed that Candelaria drank a tea of bitter orange leaves, mint, and passionflower extract every night, an ancestral recipe for good sleep.

---

[7] A rude and stupid person. Or a person of bitter, rude and generally detestable behavior.

Candelaria, who was not known to have any vices or acts at odds with the purest observance of the laws of the Holy Mother Church, only took remedies such as menthol pills to cheer herself up and, to sleep, the little tea that helped her to breathe better and have pleasant dreams, "herbal marvels" she would say when she drank it. Every night, the thick woman fell into a deep sleep that left her oblivious to noises, no matter how loud they were. But on Wednesdays, Chano liked to get fresh, with a very elegant linen guayabera to chat with his friends who dressed in shirtsleeves and alternated venues for fun games of dominoes, and to be safe from prying eyes, every Wednesday he used a double dose of tea for his brother-in-law and his beloved wife. Dadhá, on the other hand, remained in the back room and enjoyed a deep sleep. So every week, without fail, Chano was lord and master of the house, free to wander wherever he wanted, in his shirtsleeves.

That Wednesday was unforgettable. Chel stood before Chano when he added the drops to Candelaria's tea and distracted the devoted husband with a strong slap. Knowing that it was the alux, the latter began to throw punches in the air; skillfully, Chel threw some pebbles in the corner of the room, allowing Chano to grab a broom and start attacking where he supposed his opponent was. Chel took advantage and changed the contents of the cups, and Chano ended up bringing his wife an innocuous drink with a little bit of orange blossom but nothing more. Chel smiled. Candita would be a light sleeper the night Chano had planned to have a domino tournament with his illustrious friends, including the exiled doctor Maximiliano Acosta.

Everything seemed normal. Chano waited half an hour, went to his office, and turned on the dim light of a small outdoor lamp that announced the game. Chel waited patiently, and in the middle of the game, he took the opportunity to slip, without any problem, into Candelaria's room, who was sleeping restlessly. Chel jumped on her belly and shook her head, covered with a beanie. Nothing. He tried again, but this time, he slapped her face, and the woman, for the first time in years, woke up from her nightly lethargy. Chel had left open the window overlooking the courtyard that led to the master's office. The woman, raging, went to close it when she heard laughter in the distance and her husband's voice, who was supposed to be asleep at that hour. She looked up and saw the shadows of two men entering the office. The laughter and Chano's voice could be heard more clearly when the door opened. Still in disbelief, Candelaria went to the next room where her husband should be, thinking the one with the mess would be her brother, and found the bed empty.

With her walking stick in hand, she had the crowd out on the street in less than five minutes, including her husband, who was loudly protesting "my right to dress as I please and play dominoes with my friends." Candelaria just said to him.

"Go to the street, go to your friends' house, they will receive you with that look. Here, you will come back only when you have regained your decency," she said as she slammed the door in his face.

That night, when it was raining heavily, he was left alone, begging Candelaria to let him in. Wet to the bone, he went to sleep at the house of one of his colleagues with such bad luck that, as he was walking and because the street lamps were out, a cart ran over him. Hours later, he was picked up by a calash that took him to the general hospital, and he was admitted, due to his clothes and dirt, to the general ward. There, he was hospitalized with a hip, spine, several shattered bones, and a skull fracture with a severe prognosis for three months.

Candelaria suffered because the money had run out, and she had no news of her husband. When they heard from him, they sent for him to return home. Juanra devised a way to keep all of Chano's fortune and, after convincing Candelaria, conceived and carried out a plan so that the owner of the house and the money would not leave them in the street.

When he arrived, carried by two famished stretcher bearers, Chano was anxiously waiting to rest in his comfortable quarters. However, the paramedics continued to the back of the courtyard, eighty meters from the house. There, in the center of the chicken coop, Juanrá had a cardboard-walled shed erected, and in the center, his bed, his suits piled on a chair, about twenty bad books on the dirt floor, an old chamber pot and a small table with a dirty bottle of water. All the lighting consisted of a candle.

Dadhá was forbidden to go to the backyard of the house as well as the girls. Juanrá ordered a fence with barbed wire on top and three padlocks to ensure nobody could pass. The only one in charge of the space was young Jacinto. No one else, without exception, could enter the courtyard.

When evening came, the attendant told him.

—"Master, Doña Candita told me that you will not leave here until you do it on your own feet and well dressed. She forbade us to help you and appointed me your caretaker. Only I am allowed to enter. I will help you bathe once a month, bring you food at night, and empty your pot in the mornings. I am sorry."

Jacinto turned his back on him and left while the powerful landowner began crying. The doctor had predicted that he would never walk again because of the terrible fractures in both knees and his spine. He, owner of a prosperous hacienda, lord and master of lives and goods, would sleep for who knows how long, sweating, devoured by mosquitoes, in a filthy and deplorable hole with the smell of dung, humidity, garbage, and wet chickens.

When months later the pain ceased, and Christmas came, the man who, after a gifted life that cost him nothing, found himself bedridden where occasionally even the chickens laid their eggs, received a visit from Juanra who, in exchange for signing the hacienda papers, offered him better living conditions: clean sheets, coffee in the morning, more cleaning and even an electric light bulb. And if he handed over the checkbook, he could return to his room. He refused, and the food rations began to run low. The water was so dirty that he developed a merciless dysentery that kept his bed damp and stinking. Inwardly, Juanra thought, *there is nothing like time to break the toughest of men.*

One morning, as part of the "plan," Candelaria had him bathed well with aromatic soaps and clean clothes. They took him to the house, to his empty room, and fed him beans and pork as he liked, with a pitcher of fresh water and papaya jam with Dutch cheese. When they finished, Candelaria told him.

"Give me the checkbook and sign the papers, and they will bring you your bed with clean sheets," he refused. Then, they began to undress him and put on the same damp, musty, stinking clothes. He, indignant and terrified, gave in and signed Juanra's documents certifying him as the owner of all his property and all his money. Chano never left his comfortable room again, and in the hacienda and Mérida, he was presumed dead.

Once the plan was finished, Candelaria just said.

"Clean everything; now, there's plenty of room to raise a few turkeys."

And so, all at once, the memory of Eduardo Solís, whom everyone knew as the Xcau or Don Chano the terrible, was extinguished.

7

1935

When February 2nd arrived, after a *Día de Muertos* in which Chano was conspicuous by his absence at the altar, a sober and spartan Christmas, and a rather unnoticed *Día de Reyes*, the chapel that Doña Candelaria had built in honor of the virgin from whom she took her name would be inaugurated. It was Jacinto who, with his own hands, the help of a hacienda worker, and the direction of the engineer Puerto, built the small enclosure erected with the money obtained from Chano's watch and the gold coins he treasured. It was the only thing Juanra could not get hold of because it was kept in the safe, whose combination was known only to his sister. Doña Candita zealously kept her silver money and some of the jewelry she had bought from ladies in distress throughout her life. She claimed, when they knocked on her door to ask for help, that she had almost no money, that she would do it as an act of charity, although, in return, she would have to go through hardships since the hacienda was no longer generating profits since her beloved husband—who was actually in his room reading or being bored—had passed away. She asked these society women in distress to be considerate. They did not sell directly to the jeweler because their discretion was in doubt, and they preferred to sell cheaply.

Candelaria had learned from her husband to distinguish a good stone from an ordinary one with the help of a monocle that amplified the image. In addition, she had a small scale and some small bottles with different acids to classify the gold in its different purities. She was aware of the value of the precious metal because of her friendship with the family jeweler who bought the malleable metal in bulk and the diamonds and precious stones that came to her and that were not to her liking.

Father Avila would bless the premises with the bishop's permission, officiate a mass, and then preside over a dinner with delicious tamales called *vaporcitos*, good bread, and chocolate with water.

The day dawned rainy. A thunderstorm had been lashing the city since midnight, and Candita had faith that the rain would subside as the hours passed. After breakfast, she went to look out the window from where she could see the new building that housed a beautiful sapote cross with an Italian Christ, also purchased from a lady in need, and a beautiful image of the virgin that she would adorn that afternoon with some jewelry from her collection.

At one point, she thought she saw Jacinto enter the sacred precinct accompanied by a young girl who had come from the hacienda weeks before to help her family pay part of the debt at the *tienda de raya*.

The woman had a fit of rage and shouted for Juanra, who arrived with Dadhá and Chel, to witness what she was saying. They did not realize that Dadhá had seen the rain for the first time that day, at almost fifteen years old. Once accompanied, the woman took an umbrella and her iron cane, and in the middle of the storm, she went to the chapel to see that her beloved virgin and her venerated Christ were witnesses of a romantic and immoral conversation.

Her fury was so great that, without measuring the consequences, she threatened to beat the horrified boy, who protected the young girl and helped her escape in the middle of the storm. As the only safe place and with impressive agility, Jovita climbed on the weather vane that was spinning out of control. Candelaria raised her cane to order her to come down to receive her punishment when a spark from a nearby powerful lightning bolt struck the weather vane and hit Candelaria's cane. The little girl collapsed senseless from the shock on some bushes where the girls of the service ran to help her. She was badly wounded but survived.

Upon receiving the impact, Candelaria remained standing with her arm up, and the rainwater extinguished a small fire from her head. Like an automaton and given her incredible strength, with her eyes wild, she entered her house to fall flat on her face in the middle of the living room. She was in agony.

She was laid down on her bed with difficulty because the bone in her arm had fused, leaving her with a stiff limb and the cane stuck to her hand. She only managed to say that she felt very hot, so the alux moved the fan and scared the service, her brother, and Dr. Maximiliano, who came to the emergency call. When she passed away, she closed her eyes, and when he retired, Chel began to tremble with fear and told Dadhá that her soul was black and showed her that even under the storm, a vulture of the night had stood on the edge of the window. It was, he told her, the envoy of the gods who sent for her soul.

The deafening voice of the neurotic and aristocratic Juan Rafael Médici—who, during the wake of his sister Candelaria, while the corpse was still warm, decided to take her room because it was cooler—could be heard all over the house, "Keep the '*dzirits*', lest the '*hatsa há*[8]' beat it and gets wet like a month ago because of the heat wave." Dadhá, because of those absurd dictatorial measures, never went into the sea because—as her late aunt Candita warned her—it was wrong to bathe in public, and that would lead her to hell. "There is only holiness and purity after death," she constantly told her.

Dadhá's inseparable companion, Chel, witnessed her development. The alux loved honey, cuddling, discussing fashion while reading magazines, dancing, changing outfits, bathing, and talking mentally with his brother, Purutz, who told him he missed him and urged him to come back. On the other hand, he hated meat, and just as he frightened dogs, cats, opossums, birds, and snakes for fun, his terror of cockroaches made him tremble, freeze, scream, and even turn purple with fear. If he saw them from afar, he would howl like a wolf and run in terror until he got under Dadhá's clothes, to whom he would ask, trembling, to kill it. He had the habit of sitting on the girl's head, and she didn't mind because Chel weighed almost nothing. One day, on the precision scale in the apothecary's shop, Dadhá weighed Chel: the needle read twenty-one grams.

Blonde-haired, blue-eyed, short, and with a beautiful face, Dadhá was born, grew up, and died in the same house. Her only hobby was the wakes because they breathed sanctity; that and being alert when the young milkman named Salvador Del Llano, whom she imagined an incognito prince, left the four liters of "the best milk in Meérida" every morning at eight o'clock sharp, and a small piece of paper with some phrase or poem of his inspiration,

---

[8] It means water wind. It is used when it is very cloudy and the wind begins to blow, announcing that rain is coming.

which needless to say, was transmitted to him mentally, every night by Chel, according to what the girl expressed about love. If Dadhá told Chel that she would fall in love with a man who would look at her eyes and her feelings, the next day, Salvador's little paper would say something like: *A chocolate for the owner of the most beautiful eyes, of the one who only believes in feelings.*

Her day was spent between the shouts of her cantankerous father, who even grumbled at the sunrise and forced her, morning and evening, to study literature and history, especially that of the Italian monarchy, which awakened in her some fantasies about her lineage and charming princes.

Since she was a child, Dadhá was fond of praying, and since her house was right in front of the funeral home "The Afterlife," she had managed since she was fourteen years old that her father, between tantrums and tantrums and if the sky was clear, would let her go to the mass-es for the dead, her favorite. When Dadhá saw that there was movement in the funeral home, or when Chel warned her that he had seen a soul fly, she would have her black mourning dress smoothed, and when the place was already full of mourners, and always accompanied by her invisible friend, Salomé, her nanny and confidant, and her daughter Silvia, a mulatto who was getting fatter and fatter, she would cross the street and enter with the face of an or-phan to find out who the deceased was.

She liked to sit by the coffin and make an analysis of "the kind of people" that surrounded it according to the model of the coffin. She had been studying them for two years and had even seen a dead man who gave her a tide of feelings, but above all, of peace. She watched him being made up until she was invited to leave, but not without the promise that, when she was older, she would be taught how to do makeup. She knew everything about the coffins be-cause she had befriended the carpenter who worked a second shift at night, and there she would sneak out when she was not at ease in the wake. Dadhá knew everything from the quality of the wood to the ornaments. In the middle of the mourning, she would approach and see the dead person, and after caressing the ironwork and feeling the wood, she would get up and leave if it was not made of exotic wood of "high quality." If, on the other hand, it was cedar or mahogany, she would ride in mourning drama until she received the condolences. Only Father Avila would call her attention, "What you are doing, Dadhaita, is not right." She would lower her head and turn away.

Before going home, she would ask the mourners the cause of death, and once she was satis-fied with the information received, she would approach the candles and tear off some pieces of melted wax that she would put in her mouth and chew until she could swallow them. The problem for her parents was that the girl su-ffered from constant constipation, which she could only get rid of by taking castor oil. Giving it to her was a tragedy because she refused until the girls held her down on the floor and covered her nose, and when she opened her mouth, she swallowed, against her will, the disgusting remedy while Chel hid under the bed for fear that they would apply the same treatment to him.

Foresighted as she was, every time she took melted wax chips, she instructed Chel to do the same, and she would store the balls in case there was a sudden spate of communal health and an unbearable season without wakes.

"Dadhaita! Come here," shouted her mother, Trina, one hot afternoon. The young girl was rocking in her hammock, bored, looking out the window to the backyard and dreaming of her Prince Charming. She imagined the handsome nobleman jumping on his spirited steed over the high fence that guarded the house, to get off, slam the door, walk to her room, look her in the eyes, and tell her, "It's you." From there, he would kiss her while looking at the shooting stars and take her on horseback to a palace, but not before exclaiming to the four winds that Dadhá was the most beautiful woman in the universe. Her imagination made her dream of being queen and mistress of her home, the Pitti palace, of which she had drawings and even a small oil painting brought to her from Florence by Don Eugenio. And without a screaming and filthy father on the one hand and a controlling and apparently submissive mother on the other, dedicated to collecting strange things of art.

Her coronation as the great princess of Mérida, she told Chel, who listened with fascination, would outshine those of European royalty. She would be seen in an uncovered golden palanquin with her prince, always a little behind her, strolling through the cobblestone center of Mérida, people throwing flowers at her, spraying gallons of delicate French perfume in the streets and holding her portrait aloft, as well as the little flags with the Médici anagram, waving, as in her homeland in the past in the hands of the children who wept with emotion at the sight of her. Later, she would move to Progreso to take her beloved's luxurious yacht, a brigantine faster than the wind, named Dadhá in her honor, and head for Florence, where crowds would be waiting for her at the foot of her palace to cheer her on. There, they would name her the Grand Duchess of Tuscany. She would arrive at her chambers carried in the arms of her beloved, and they would live, amidst cakes and champagne, eternally happy. She would, of course, bestow the same title of duke on her beloved.

"Dadhaaaaaa, come here!" Trina shouted again. "I have to tell you something! What a stubborn child, undoubtedly thinking of extravagances," she said quietly.

Trina instructed one of the girls to call her and tell her that Doña Elena Mier and her daughter Bertita, who had just arrived from Paris, were with her and were bringing her some gifts.

Reluctantly, Dadhá came out of her reverie, put on a house dress, and went, dragging her feet and pushed by Chel, who kept telling her, "They brought us a little present, hurry up, ninia, they are leaving." Upon reaching the living room, she found the mother and daughter elegantly dressed and waiting for her. Both in pink, the mother in burnt pink, the daughter in pastel pink with lace that seemed avant-garde to Dadhá.

"Here, I brought you these magazines from Paris," said Bertita, happy to see her friend. They began to leaf through them, and Dadhá asked Trina for permission to go out to the terrace where a cool breeze had started to blow after a scorching day when the weather vane had not moved. Now, it was brightening the atmosphere with its cadenced chirping. On the terrace were four chairs and a small cast iron table painted white, and on the sides were some rare pots in the shape of Dutch Swedes that Trina had bought from an emerging artist. These were filled with plants and flowers, from bougainvillea to tulips.

There, under the colorful light of the sunset, Dadhá got to know *Vogue* magazine, French fashion, and black lingerie presented by designer Paul Poiret. Among the photos was a bra, the latest French invention, which supported and lifted the bust. Her friend Bertita told her she was wearing one, unleashing a frenzy in the little Médici girl who only said.

"I want a black one for my fifteenth birthday present; I'll ask my mother for it," and just then, at the Médici residence, "the war for French clothes" began.

"No! It's not up for discussion. I won't buy you French clothes as if we were millionaires!"

That was Dadhá's father's response when she showed him the magazine images her friend Bertita had just given her.

"But Daddy, I'm almost fifteen years old, and you know I don't like white clothes, and the ones I wear now are for little girls. Look, talk it over with my mom; she understands me," she shouted for the first time to a man who was used to shouting even at the rain for getting him wet.

Her mother, after arguing sourly with her stubborn husband, told him.

"This is going to have consequences, you know Dadhá. She is so angry that she could get sick." The father repeated, making a face of annoyance.

"Noooo, don't insist; I won't spend a single penny."

It was strictly forbidden to enter Don Juanrá's library in the Médici residence when he was not present. The ill-tempered writer didn't like anyone entering his library except for the young maid who cleaned it. He allowed her to be in the library for a few minutes each week.

Chel told his friend about the conversation, and she told the alux.

"I hope I get sick so that my father suffers but of something serious so that he gets scared," the alux told her.

"In this life, you have to be or appear to be. You can get sick without being sick."

"What do you mean?" his friend asked.

"Yes, purge yourself and make up that you feel much worse than you actually do."

And how could things be that one of those strange afternoons and breaking his habit of not leaving his house, Juanra attended the wake of a very close friend of his, Dr. Laviada, who, together with his son Fernandito, visited them every time an illness came to his home. The curmudgeon reluctantly dusted off his mourning frock coat and, with his gelled hair and his face washed, put on the uncomfortable suit that had already seen its best days and reluctantly crossed Sixty-fifth Street, which at that time was paved with what the merchant ships transported as ballast. During that time, ships would bring roof tiles and cobblestones to Progreso. These materials were provided upon request by the mayors of Mérida. The ships would then fill their holds with bales of henequen, which was a way for them to cover their expenses for the trip and stabilize the pilot's boats.

That afternoon, Dadhá, against her habit of not missing any funeral, was "sick to her stomach." That morning, the seller of sweet oranges had passed by. Trina, who liked to drink juice every morning, bought a hundred oranges from the seller. Dadhá was aware of the harmful effects of consuming too many oranges, so she took twenty of those fruits on a morning when the heat wave was intense, and she had also taken a spoonful of olive oil with aniseed magnesia, a powerful laxative used only in cases of severe constipation. She told Mari she would not go, which surprised her father, who knew of her taste for funerals and his daughter's esteem for Dr. Laviada.

To the teenager's surprise, her father entered her room and lavished some tender words on her.

"Are you sick, Dadhaíta? I don't want any scares. Behave yourself! I'm worried and can't write poems like this, and Nicho ordered me one and even gave me an advance! I'm going to see the doctor for the last time; he wasn't so good after all, he still told me last week about his plans to go to Europe. He didn't see his death coming."

As her parents left, she realized that, strangely enough, she was alone with the housekeeper. After running to the bathroom for the eighth time, she passed through the airtight office and noticed that, in his haste, the curmudgeon had not, as was his custom, taken the trouble to lock his door. Gathering her strength and after checking that no one was watching her, she entered the dark, stinking library.

She felt a shiver, more from the diarrhea than from the stench of tobacco and sweat, and began to look through the bookcases that, crammed with documents, old newspapers, and, of course, manuscripts, filled every corner of the dimly lit and sinister room.

She was already on her way out, more out of fear than lack of interest, when her sight stumbled upon a voluminous book that her father used to consult, together with the recently deceased physician, dated nineteen hundred and twenty, *Bertillon, Compendium of diseases and their morbidity*. Without further ado, a smile lit up her face. In seconds, she had concocted the Machiavellian plan of a resentful girl. She hugged the volume and, without anyone seeing her, ran to her room, hid it under the mattress of her bed, and ran back to the bathroom for the ninth time.

Already in her room and accompanied by Chel, whom she had already taught to read Spanish, they found that a dangerous disease of unknown origin, hepatitis, could be fatal. They carefully read the list of symptoms; she memorized them, and on her way to the bathroom for the tenth time, she left the old tome in the office with the ribbon on the page of the disease to be invented.

"Let's see," she said to Chel, "jaundice. That, I read, is to be yellow." The alux, who had a prodigious memory, jumped up and said, dancing with joy, "I know, I know, I know. Let me tell you something: when your uncle Chano had his meal, and I pulled his wig off, a Spanish cook came and made a yellow rice casserole. She used something called saffron to get the color we need. Your mom has stored several little jars; I don't think she'll notice if a few are missing. I remember the woman at the fancy meal telling her daughters to be careful not to get any broth in the rice because it had saffron and "it was a stain."

And he continued, very proud of his plan.

"Now that your parents are out, you're going to take a bath," the alux ran to the kitchen and returned with a container of the exotic yellow pistils in a few minutes. He prepared the hot tub for her, for which he had to fill the modern chip heater and turn it on, and when the water was at its hottest, he filled the tub and poured part of the small bottle of saffron. Within seconds, the tub was tinted yellow. He pulled Dadhá, who was fainting, in for a bath and said to her, "Dive in and open your eyes as wide as you can because they have to turn yellow, too."

Trina's fright was great when, in the morning and after hearing Dadhá go to the bathroom a few times, she found her sprawled on her bed with sunflower-colored skin. She gave a scream that woke up the father, who crossed the street to request the services of Dr. Max Acosta, who had been banned from the house for fifteen years. The doctor found an obvious case of hepatitis and even more because Dadhá screamed when she was auscultated in the liver area. He also asked her about her stool, and she lied.

"White." "Your urine?" "Dark."

"It's very clear," the doctor said with a worried face, "she has hepatitis. The girl must eat fat-free foods and lots of sweets, jams, honey, and sugar for two months. Nothing salty or irritating. Ah, she has to rest completely." Chel danced with happiness. They had fooled the doctor.

And Dadhá was busy talking about her imminent death and eating poorly—in appearance—since Chel was bringing her food on the sly. Her mother, distressed, asked her what to do for her. She would only say that she would die because she had no reason to live. Finally, after a few weeks of torturing her mother, she told her point-blank, "The only thing I would have liked was to have French clothes." Trina said to her that if she ate well, she would, with or without permission, order a couple of French dresses and a brassiere from her friend Mimi Bolio, who was about to leave for New Orleans for two weeks. "Well," said Dadhá, "a pair of Parisian sunglasses would cheer me up." And Trina complied. Magically, Dadhá, who stopped giving herself saffron baths, improved in just a few days, just enough to receive her longed-for garments without her father noticing. "You have to be or appear to be," Chel repeated to her with satisfaction.

"If that's how you want them to be, all material things are what they seem," Chel told Dadhá such a famous phrase when she was unpacking the French clothes and the little box with the fashionable glasses that had just arrived from New Orleans.

"Make sure your father doesn't notice, or he'll make such a fuss that the Pastry War will be a child's game," her mother warned. She had already given in to her daughter's manipulations.

In addition to ordering the girl's clothes to please her and managing the house's running, Trina was dedicated to promoting culture, particularly Dadaist art manifestations, among her friends and acquaintances. She, too, had ordered a fashionable set of clothes, a pair of glasses, and a tailored suit from a new designer who had rebelled against the 19th-century clothes she called antique. November 2nd, *Día de Muertos* was approaching, and Dadhá's eternal companion and accomplice had found a way to manipulate Trina by talking to her when she was falling asleep, imitating her voice. He would do it in a sweet but firm tone, almost imperceptible so that when she woke up, the lady of the house would believe that it had occurred to her. So, for example, if Chel or Dadhá wanted to eat chocolate cake, Chel would sneak into Trina's room, and on the back of Justino, the lizard, would climb into her bed and say.

"Tomorrow, when you wake up, you will have the wonderful idea of having a chocolate cake made with delicious cocoa from the United States. No eggs because they are bad for you. You will invite Bertita and her mother to talk about fashion." He repeated this until she smiled and fell asleep. The next day, Dadhá and Chel would eat cake, and in the afternoon, they would get ready to skim through European art and fashion magazines with her friend.

Trina had no limits when she had a taste for the most exotic fashion. Proof of this was the pigeon-bodied shoes she wore on special occasions. They were practically a replica of the body of a pigeon and, on the toe, a stuffed head of the bird. She also bought strange objects, and her house looked like a Dada art museum.

The day the package arrived was an important day: Dadhá would go out again, fully restored, with French clothes and her beloved fashionable glasses. They would go to the funeral home. Chel knew this early in the morning because he had seen a white soul pass through the sky to meet the bereaved. When that happened, the alux went into a trance, as usual, and after a few minutes of total immobility, he said to Dadhá.

"There is movement today, have your dress ready; a young man died."

And indeed, at about three o'clock in the afternoon, the carriage of the funeral home, "The Afterlife," was ready and loaded with a coffin to go for the deceased.

Dadhá, who had already developed a taste for perfumes, soaps, and expensive creams, had devised a source of financing because her miserly father did not spend on anything but things for himself. Looking out the window as the coffin was being loaded, she crossed over and looked it over with some indifference. She noticed that it was of good quality without being the best and prepared her strategy. She asked Don Adolfo, the coachman, where they would go to pick him up, to which he replied.

"Nearby, girl, by the corner of the little elephant."

That was an area of middle-class homes. She already had the information she needed. Se would just have to watch out for Father Avila.

"Juanra," said Trina to her husband, "today I'm going to Sixty-fourth Street to a committee meeting for the Festival of the Dead. We are going to decide where to put the altar this year. I think we have a good chance that it will be here because we are already considered part of society because of how well-decorated the house is. Today, it will be at the Palomino's house, people of the highest lineage. They are the same people building a bullring replica of the Bullring of Toledo. It will be a jewel on the outskirts of the city. And they consider us their equals; they are modest but very cultivated people."

"Shut up now!" replied the ill-tempered man. "You behave more and more like my deceased sister Candelaria."

"Oh, by the way, I have authorized Dadhá to go to mass and to give comfort to the parents of the young boy who died because he climbed up to free his parrot from the weather vane of his house. They are good people; his father is a notary public of notary office six—modest but hard-working people."

"Are you telling me or asking me?" asked the man in a challenging manner.

Trina did not answer; she just said.

"See you later."

That day, like every Monday, Mérida smelled of boiled beans with epazote. In most houses, beans with pork would be eaten.

The bean was the fascination of Chel, who, not being used to meat, suffered from gas in abundance and eliminated it in a single exhibition, causing dizziness and fainting to anyone who was near because of its strange origin. They fell according to the intensity. After eating the dish that afternoon, he lay down to sleep on a branch of the tamarind tree, playing with a squirrel. He could hardly move, and his stomach was distending. At about four o'clock, when the family gathered for coffee, Dadhá missed Chel. She looked out on the terrace and saw him lying on the lowest branch. She went to look for him, carried him affectionately to bring him into the house, and said.

"It looks like your belly is going to explode. You're a big eater; you eat more than your brother Purutz," to which the alux made an embarrassed face.

As soon as she sat down, just as her father was being served coffee, Chel let out a long moan, which everyone could hear, something like ten cicadas, and let out, all at once, all the stinking blue air. Everyone, including Dadhá, passed out for a few minutes. His fumes were a secret weapon.

And then came the long-awaited moment. Dadhá took a long bubble bath, shaved her legs, waxed her whole body, and put on her clothes in the French fashion. As if it were a ritual, she stroked the dress below her knees to check for wrinkles and slowly put it on. She looked in the mirror and saw that it looked good on her and, for the first time, she liked herself.

When she finished, she looked out the window and saw that her relatives and friends were already gathering. What surprised her the most was the presence of young Salvador, the milkman, bathed and dressed in an old suit, looking at the door of her house. As she left the house, swaying to the rhythm of some imaginary modern music—and with Chel following closely—wearing her new glasses, she decided to walk around the block, followed by two service girls who always accompanied her.

Without wasting any time, Chavita crossed the sidewalk and greeted her.

"Miss, how nice to see you. I imagined you were going to young Luis' wake today."

"And how did you know?" she asked, smiling and adjusting her glasses so that they looked.

The boy took a breath, told her he was making the last milk delivery at the now deceased's house, and witnessed the accident.

"Did he die immediately, or was he taken to the hospital?" she asked.

"He fell on his head; it was instantaneous. He lay there. A tragedy, may I accompany you?" Dhada thought about it and said to him.

"We'd better meet inside; I have a lot to talk about with the bereaved and friends," she turned around and went inside, moved as if she were the widow.

The boy had not yet been taken to the wake room; he was being prepared in the back room. She sneaked into the room where the mortician was doing his makeup and asked him to let her help him, to which he agreed when he saw such a beautiful and fashionable young lady. He said to her.

"Don't spend a lot of makeup; they ordered the cheapest package. You can tell they are middle class."

That was enough. Dadhá returned to the room and quickly surveyed the crowd. She identified the mourners and friends and told Chel who she thought each one was. In the back, seated in very comfortable armchairs, was a very elegant couple. She found her target! She approached them, introduced herself as a family friend, and explained the hardships the relatives endured to pay for the burial, especially since their dignity did not allow them to ask for help.

"Do not say another word!" said the thick personage with the face of good people. He took out twenty silver pesos and gave them slyly to Dadhá, who thanked him and then went to the family. She gave them her condolences and told them that the gentleman, who was leaving at that moment, had ordered a beautiful wreath, but he did not want it to be known. The grieving father managed to raise his hand in thanks. The woman saw him and said.

"Ah, he's my husband's boss—a good man."

Dadhá approached Chavita, who kept looking at her, and after exchanging a couple of sentences with him, she asked him if he could go to the flower shop next door and order a pretty wreath of three pesos. He said yes, and Dadhá gave him the money. Upon receiving it, the boy said.

"Now I'll take care of it and then I'm leaving; I've already seen you," and blushing, he added, "you are very pretty and elegant; you dress very elegantly. See you tomorrow."

The girl turned to Chel and said.

"I already have enough for the French perfume; tomorrow, I'll order it for the first one who travels," she laughed cynically. Her eternal companion asked if they could bring him even a cheap cologne. Dadhá nodded and affirmed that they would bring him the best.

Meanwhile, two blocks away, Trina was put in charge of the altar that would be presented at a traditional mucbipollos dinner. Each person would bring either a pib or a good loaf of bread, and the husbands and older children would attend the celebration. It was agreed to compensate Father Avila for his services in celebrating a rosary for the souls in purgatory, and the altar would be unveiled. It would be the following Monday, November 2nd, at six o'clock in the afternoon.

At the Medici house, everything was chaos. As soon as he heard the racket, Juanrá made himself comfortable in what was once Chano's office. He sat down in the envied armchair and said quietly, looking into the next room.

"You see, Chanito, you can't leave your room, and I own all your goods. And for a plate of food and five cents worth of sulfa, ha, ha, ha, ha, ha," The writer laughed loudly, revealing his yellow and decaying teeth. His mouth was nearly toothless.

In the great hall, with Chel as a witness who did not miss any detail to inform Dadhá, who was sleeping peacefully, a *Hanal Pixán* of seven trim levels began to be assembled. The ritual with tremendous syncretic value represented the seven Mayan heavens on one side and, on the highest part, a Catholic cross. Small pots with copal burning in charcoal, candles, offerings, food, alcohol, cigarettes, images, saints, and yellow Mayan tajonal flowers combined with European flowers resulted in an unexpected burst of color and beliefs.

Everything was perfect. Everyone thought so, both the Mayan housekeepers and Trina, a woman of French descent with eclectic taste.

Everyone thought it was wonderful. The women set up a translucent curtain that would be drawn before dinner, with the lights off so that the candles of the offering would stand out.

In the kitchen, two mucbipollos were prepared, a large baked tamal filled with chicken and meat, with one hundred percent Mayan recipes and accompanied by a citrus salad with habanero, hot chocolate with water and sugar, and delicious European bread. The gastronomic fusion was present in every detail. And Trina and the Yucatecan society loved it.

When Dadhá woke up, she first looked at the altar, which she found "nice" but bland, just like Chel. Something was missing. After exchanging glances, they both smiled and said in unison, "Let's get to work!"

The two disappeared for a long time until they were summoned for lunch.

"Don't eat too many beans, Chel, remember that it has pork, even if you put it on the side."

Chel listened to Dadhá in everything except eating beans from the pot every Monday. The alux, after a long morning of work that included several outings, ate to his heart's content. In addition, while they worked on the sly, Dadhá and he had drunk a liter of tamarind water pre-pared for the night. Although it was November, the heat was unbearable. In the middle of the morning's work, Dadhá began to talk with Chavita about a thousand and one things, and the conversation under the sun went on for half an hour, during which they both sweated. They agreed to see each other at the next wake. She thanked him for the beautiful wreath and unex-pectedly received a humble silver cross as a gift from the young milkman.

"For you to wear it tonight, you're going to look beautiful," he told her. She blushed, and he blushed too.

The guests, belonging to the wealthiest Yucatecan society, arrived at half past six in shiny luxury automobiles. "The street was filled with high class," said Trina, who was already dreaming of her daughter married to some millionaire heir from a European county, looking out the window. The four tables of ten were filled immediately. Jacinto, dressed in a frock coat he had rescued from "the late Chano's" estate, had on white gloves and a pair of shoes, also inherited, but which were too big for him, was sweating profusely. The suits were already light-colored, and the women were beginning to leave the long dresses behind. Three-quarter skirts were in fashion. Only a few older ladies showed up in long skirts. The servers served and poured refreshments while twenty liters of chocolate were heated in the kitchen.

Mrs. Perfecta Palomino came to the front to welcome the distinguished concurrence, "the most distinguished of society." While she said a few words about the event, Trina asked Dadhá to select a potential candidate from the attendees. It was frowned upon to remain a bachelor at eighteen. A young man with decent looks stared at her intensely and even introduced himself.

"I am Álvaro Treviño. Could I visit you sometime?"

"Let me think about it," she said dryly, "I'll answer you later."

And while the president of the Friendship Club was naming everyone present, Chel was working busily behind the scenes. At that moment, a girl on duty received the order to light the candles that Chel had already lit. She told her mistress they were already lit and didn't know who did it. Doña Perfecta applauded for what would be the best altar in Mérida and called Trina to come forward to unveil the offering.

The lights were turned off, and the curtain was drawn back amidst a total silence that turned into strange voices and, finally, into screams of horror. At the highest part of the altar, and in the style of Mayan funerals, a half-naked dead man with bristling hair and a dreadful smile crowned the *Hanal Pixán*. At that moment, and because so many beans had been eaten that day, fermented with tamarind, a kind of buzzing of a thousand cicadas began to be heard amidst the screams. And *bam*! All of a sudden, Chel's belly deflated, emitting a blue *kiis*, and everyone except Dadhá, who had seen him eating rampantly and had put a clothespin on her nose, fell down, fainting from the horrible stench.

Dadhá realized that their idea had not been a good one, and with the help of Chel's enormous strength, they dragged the dead man out and hid him in the henhouse. In minutes, they put everything as it was so that, when they woke up, the guests would not see the corpse that, a few seconds before the flatulence of the alux, had begun to burn from the head due to the proximity of one of the candles.

Everyone awoke from their lethargy, and upon seeing the altar just as Trina had left it, they decided it had been a collective suggestion. Without further ado, they set about eating the delights of Yucatecan cuisine.

8

"Jovita," said Trina to Dadhá's new helper.

"This child is very lazy. The teacher, Carmita, arrives at eight o'clock, and Dadhá makes her wait every day. She has to discipline herself because they charge me for four hours. Then, at noon, Don Vittorio comes, and since they haven't finished their lessons, the Italian classes are getting shorter. From now on, you are responsible for Dadhá to wake up at half past six, take a bath, have breakfast, and be ready for class. If she is late again, tell her she will not be able to attend the masses for the dead. And I will return you to the hacienda."

Jovita, who had already learned to detect Chel's presence by the smell of wet earth and tamarind blossom, became aware of his presence and told Trina.

"Tell Chel, who is over there, to help because he is lazier. He just wants to sleep with Dadhá, and when she is in class, he goes to loaf in the trees or to ride Justino, but he is the first one ready to go to mass. And the first one to sit down to eat."

Trina looked at him and answered.

"Do you expect me to talk to an imaginary friend or a being from beyond the grave or whatever you want to call it?"

"Jovita, the teacher Carmita told me yesterday that Dadhá is absent a lot. She goes to the bathroom or to take her medicine, and it takes her hours to come back. Just yesterday, the teacher told me she went to 'freshen up' and it took her over half an hour!"

From that moment on, the young woman devoted herself to torturing her young mistress. At twenty-past six, she awoke, climbed down from the hammock next to Dadhá's bed, washed her face in the new moon-like sink, and began the struggle. First, she set about sniffing to locate Chel by his smell. Once she discovered the alux, she began to grope in the gloom and felt a tingling sensation, followed by a strange chuckle. She was actually tickling the alux's head, which, hatless, presented a frizzy, standing hair.

"Chel," she said, "please wake up and help me lift this dormouse. If you do, I promise to give you the jar of honey that they always hide in the kitchen. They suspect one of us is eating it, but I know where Doña Salomé keeps it."

Upon saying that about the honey, the woman saw Dadhá's pillow sink slightly, her face began to contort, and she saw her hair being pulled. After a few minutes of futilely struggling with her, the activity ceased, but suddenly, she saw the glass of water on Dadhá's bedside table float through the air until it was on top of her face. Jovita shouted quietly to Chel not to do that, but it was too late. The contents fell on the peaceful face of Dadhá, who jumped up and asked why she was being woken up like that. Her assistant showed her the moving glass, and Dadhá scolded the alux.

"The laziness is over! You woke me up, but you don't dare move from my side in class so that you'll get over your dumbness. No more lazing around in the tamarind tree or swallowing fruit all day; you're already fatter than a cistern!"

When the teacher Carmita Rodriguez, a plump woman in her fifties, whiter than white, entered the study room, a well-ventilated room facing the side of the house and the street, from where Dadhá spied on the movements of the funeral home, she found her impeccably dressed, bathed and combed. In front of her was her notebook and, to one side, her books. The morning passed slowly. At one point, the young girl asked the teacher for permission to go to the bathroom, and as she left, like a sentinel, Jovita was waiting to accompany her.

"Don't you have anything to do?" she demanded.

"Yes, see that you don't fall asleep."

Dragging her feet, she went to the bathroom and sat on the toilet to fall asleep... for a minute, until the knocking on the door of her now guardian woke her up. Dadhá was groggy from sleep when she came out of the bathroom, so the young woman in charge of keeping her awake grabbed her by the wrists, dragged her to the sink, and poured fresh water on her. Nothing. She was starting to fall asleep while standing until Trina came in, gave her a knock on the head, and shouted at her.

"Go to study, and that's the end of it!"

She didn't nod off again from the scare for ten minutes but spent the whole morning thinking of a way to sleep. She would hide behind her big notebook and pretend she was writing something down, and Chel would pull her head up by her hair. It was immense torture. Besides, it was Monday, the day she was taking Italian lessons from Professor Vittorio. It was the most boring hour of the day. The sixty-year-old man, thin as paper, with an aquiline nose, dressed in an old gray suit, a bun around his neck, and a bad toupee, would start his classes the same way. He counted from one to one hundred in Italian and then went over countless simple sentences. When Dadhá gave the first signs of falling asleep, at about half past twelve, the teacher pounded the ruler and began to scold Dadhá, who started to cry. The anger was greater than Chel's strength. No one, no one made his friend cry without consequences. After becoming enraged, he got down from the table to his friend's concern, who called him slyly. Chel did not listen to reasons; he was furious. He climbed on Don Vittorio's head, took off his glasses, poked his eyes, tore off his toupee, hung on the bow tie, and gave him while falling, a kick in the crotch. All in a second. The professor, in shock, sat down on a chair and asked.

"What happened?"

Chel began to throw the books at him, and the teacher decided that he was before some evil entity and after peeing himself with fear, he ran away, never to return, to the laughter of Dadhá and the apologies of Trina, who tried to stop him to which he replied, "I don't know, I don't know." Trina noticed his wet pants and laughed. Don Vittorio was never heard from again.

Her mother looked at her and told her.

"Dadaíta, for doing I don't know what to the teacher, today you will embroider with me all afternoon. No naps."

"But Mom," she said, "there's going to be a wake today; an acquaintance of mine died of dysentery."

"Well," answered Trina, "you finish the embroidered collar that you haven't stitched for a week, or you won't go." And the girl embroidered well and fast, like an angel.

As she was going to see Salvador, she put on some color and took her mother's lipstick. Silvia, who had ironed her funeral dress, said.

"Only your visits to funeral homes keep you awake."

"I don't think so; I can't keep my eyes open. But I'm meeting Chavita. Besides, I want to see Malenita one last time. She wasn't a close friend, but I've known her since childhood."

When she went out, she met Alvarito, who hovered around her day and night. He was carrying a bouquet, which she despised.

And without further ado, she left him standing where he was to cross the street and enter the funeral home.

In the back room, the deceased young woman was lying on the table destined to arrange the dead. Dadhá approached her and, dizzy from sleep, saw that she was very thin, dressed in black, and had been placed on the right side. One side remained half empty. She measured it with her eyes and thought, *no one should be denied a little nap. It would be an hour before they take her out and before Chava arrives.* She lightly painted her lips and lay down next to her acquaintance. Chel, who wanted to lie down because he had not been allowed to sleep either, forced himself in between the two, and when Dadhá was already sound asleep, as never before, the alux gave a hip thrust that threw the deceased to the floor, between the blankets with which she had been covered for her transfer. After a while, the assistants of the funeral home arrived, brought the coffin closer, and saw Dadhá. They said between them, "Look, what a pity, it is the girl who comes a lot." They took her feet and shoulders and put her in the coffin, which they proceeded to take to the wake.

When the lid was opened amid the large group of mourners and attendants, loud voices of "she is not the one, she is not the one" were heard. The commotion woke up the sleepy young woman. When she opened her eyes, she smiled and apologized before getting out of the coffin to check her clothes. With a firm step, she left, giving a flirtatious salute to Chava, who could not understand what was happening. Two women fainted, and several had nervous breakdowns, which was the result of Dadhá Médici De Pablo's best and most peaceful siesta.

As the months passed, Dadhá kept talking with Chavita at each wake. On more than one occasion, Salvador saw Alvarito standing at the doors of his beloved's house until Salvador asked her, and she only told him, "A nuisance; I don't know how to get rid of him."

The routine was the same: when there was going to be a ceremony, Dadhá knew beforehand, so during her morning meeting with the milkman, she would take the opportunity to tell him, "Look, today is going to be the funeral of so-and-so's mother or father or uncle. I'm very sad." Salvador, who was not very bright, did not notice the insinuation but mysteriously heard a little inner voice telling him.

"Don't be silly, today you can see her in the evening... bring her chocolateeeeeeees."

The well-built young man smiled, and as soon as he finished delivering a hundred liters of milk, he went to buy some sweets and after his nap, he groomed himself with special care. He had been collecting money for a second-hand black suit that the tailor was selling him, and he finally bought it.

One of those afternoons, when there was a wake, Chavita showed up with his new "*flus*" and an ironed shirt. Dadhá was impressed to see him in black. Tall, not ugly at all, with humble chocolates. She was sure he was an incognito prince and told Chel so. He laughed and inspired, he blurted out.

"Chavita is not of nobility, but if he considers you the queen of his world, he will be the prince you are waiting for. If he makes you feel like you are in the clouds, any house will be a palace. If he gives you his heart, it will be more precious than the most fabulous jewel. And if he makes your heart flutter, he will be the love of your life. Whether he is a cow owner or a landowner, it doesn't matter. If he is a worker, which he is, he himself is a jewel and should be worth to you."

Dadhá was speechless. She ran to the window and, upon seeing him, expressed with emotion.

"He's my prince, I'm in love."

That afternoon, at the wake, Dadhá, after entering the back room and helping to make up the dead man and cutting a curl of his hair for her collection, approached the candles from which she pulled a bit of melted wax, offered condolences to the mourners on behalf of the Yucatecan society, and sat down on the chairs in the back next to Salvador. This time, she left out the sarcasm and allowed herself to compliment Salvador on his attire and even said to him.

"You look very distinguished; you look European." He explained that he was descended from Norwegian immigrants, which explained why he was so big and hardworking. In an outburst, and just when they were taking the deceased to the living room and the relatives burst into tears, Salvador asked her, with one knee on the floor, if she would like to be his beloved and handed Dadhá a little brown bag with cheap chocolates. Chel grimaced with displeasure because he liked the stuffed truffles. She said yes, stood up, and he hugged her happily while the others cried.

During the night, Chel had "worked" Juanrá by telling him while he was dozing that Dadhá had mystic powers and should be feared.

He repeated it until it changed the face of the ill-tempered man, who fell asleep with a look of terror.

Chel and his friend hatched a plan: she would tell her dad about Salvador, and the alux would spring into action when he said no. To do this, Chel slipped in with the neurotic father and climbed up, cloaked in his invisibility, right before him.

"Dad," Dadhá said, staring at him, "I am Salvador's girlfriend; he proposed to me yesterday at the wake."

"The milkman?" her father shouted.

"Yes, he is very hardworking and handsome."

"Over my dead body!" he replied.

And just as they had planned, Dadhá stared at him with a furious face, and just then, glasses, cups, pictures, and papers began to fly all over the writer's office. Trembling with fear, the frantic father turned into a little lamb and whispered.

"Okay, fine, marry whoever you want, but don't practice witchcraft anymore."

She theatrically raised her hand, and the destructive "event" stopped.

"I'm only going to ask you two things, Dad, that you tell my mom and that you allow me to receive visits from Salvador. Oh, and that you talk to him sometime."

He was going to refuse, but at that moment, Dadhá began to raise her hand as if to unleash her fury, and in a split second, he nodded. He surrendered unconditionally and sat sprawled on the worn leather couch.

Two years later, Dadhá and Salvador's marriage suddenly erased the family's dreams of belonging to the nobility, and they had to make do with what a dozen zebu cows on the outskirts of Mérida produced.

For their wedding night, Salvador, after receiving three canes from his future father-in-law, just for the hell of it, was instructed, in a family conclave, with the presence of the priest and without Dadhá's assistance, of course, on how he should behave. She and her aunt Loreto and her mother Trinidad were busily embroidering the bride's headdress. Meanwhile, in the great library of the mediocre writer and poet, they were sentencing the one who, somewhat out of contempt, was nicknamed Chavita.

"After the wedding, you will go on honeymoon to the hacienda, and Silvia will accompany you."

The wedding, with the best of the Yucatecan society, was celebrated in the cathedral with a large turnout. The highlight was the bride, who appeared in a spectacular black dress, headdress, and bouquet. Unfortunately, they could not see Chel, dressed in a full dress, bowler hat, and bow tie. He told her he would leave for a few days to visit his family and brother Purutz after the wedding. He also mentioned that he would be practicing Kimbomba during his trip because he had plans to compete that year when Kukulkán would come down. However, he assured her that he would be back soon.

The celebration at the Medici home included an eight-course banquet, music with a lone violinist who roamed downtown Mérida playing for tips, and two separate sections of tables: in the front for the bride's guests and in the back, halfway across the courtyard, for the groom's relatives, rowdies who stood out with their uncontrolled laughter.

Dadhá was dancing with Salvadorito to songs of the time, and a dozen couples were accompanying them. Suddenly, she felt a hand touching her shoulder. It was Chel turned human. He explained to her that he had found a golden mushroom inside the Xibal and had been able to convert for a while. The effect would be short-lived, and he could only do it once in his life, and that was the moment his friend chose for it. They danced twist until the effect passed, and Salvador took his place.

Shortly after that, Trina beckoned to her.

—Mira —le dijo—, ya se va tu amigo.

"Look," she said, "your friend is leaving."

Dadhá, bewildered, looked back and saw Chel already as an alux, with his little bundle, heading for the well from where he would sail to Xibal. Surprised, Dadhá opened her eyes wide and asked her mother.

"Can you see him too?"

Trina smiled as Chel turned around and waved goodbye to both mother and daughter.

To be continued...

Index

7
85

8
107

www.ingramcontent.com/pod-product-compliance
Lightning Source LLC
Chambersburg PA
CBHW051129160726
47997CB00018B/868